Abigail

"Those are oranges, Susan."

Abigail

By
PORTIA HOWE SPERRY
and
LOIS DONALDSON

Pictured by
ZABETH SELOVER

Second Edition
Edited and revised by Barbara J. Dirks

INDIANA HISTORICAL SOCIETY
Indianapolis 2000

Second printing, September, 1939

Reprinted by the Indiana Historical Society, 2000

Barbara J. Dirks wrote the introduction and changed the text to remove archaic language.

CONTENTS

ABIGAIL

FULL PAGE ILLUSTRATIONS

BLACK AND WHITE PLATES

ABIGAIL

To

A. J. ROGERS,

whose encouragement made possible

our work in Brown County.

To

H V D, G F A, and M McE,

who were with me on the motor trip

which made this book possible.

ABIGAIL

ABIGAIL

ABIGAIL

INTRODUCTION

Abigail is set at the time of American expansion west of the Alleghenies. In this book the Tom Calvin family leaves its farm in Kentucky for a fresh start in the new state of Indiana. The Treaty of St. Marys, signed in 1818, opened up what is now the central third of the state for settlement. Calvin's brother Sam had already moved his family to Brown County, Indiana, and as with many families, his letters to relatives back in Kentucky encouraged more of the family to migrate to Indiana too.

Early Indiana settlers traveled by foot and covered wagon, following the same route from Kentucky to Indiana over dirt roads through the Kentucky wilderness to the Ohio River. They experienced the difficult decision of determining what to take and what to leave behind. Families heading into Indiana crossed the Ohio River at Madison, Indiana, which was nicknamed "The Gateway to the State." Readers learn how pioneer families worked together to build homes in the Indiana wilderness and how neighbors worked and celebrated together.

ABOUT THE AUTHORS

Author Portia Howe Sperry moved from Allen County to Brown County, Indiana, with her family because of the Great Depression and a family illness. In Fort Wayne her husband owned a very successful business, and they shared a beautiful home with their four children. When the depression came in 1929 the family lost everything. Their business had to close, and no one had the money to buy it. Mr. Sperry became ill and was unable to look for work. The family eventually decided to take its possessions and move to Brown County, Indiana. They had happy memories of a Brown County vacation and were sure their father would get well again if they moved there. They lived in two wooden shacks until they found a rather rundown place to live outside of Nashville. They were able to repair the house as part of their rent.

Mrs. Sperry found work at the Nashville House, a hotel there in town, and later was asked to manage its gift shop. The store owner wanted

"Oh Grandmother, here's a doll."

to feature items that were handcrafted in the area and hoped she would develop some ideas. She designed a cloth doll, patterned after the rag dolls her daughters loved, and named it Abigail. Mrs. Sperry traveled around the community showing local women how to make the dolls so they could work in their homes and earn extra money to help their families. The dolls were educational toys as their clothing had buttons, snaps, and shoelaces to tie. Their hair was made of cut fabric so little girls could learn to make braids. Mrs. Sperry hoped that children would learn to dress themselves as they learned to dress the doll. Abigail dolls became so popular they were sold at Marshall Field's Department Store in Chicago.

As a result of this popularity Mrs. Sperry and Lois Donaldson wrote this story about Abigail, making the book educational and related to Nashville, Indiana, as well as entertaining. Their efforts resulted in an historically accurate tale describing how families migrated from Kentucky to Indiana in the early 1800s.

CHAPTER I.

ABIGAIL ARRIVES

"SUSAN," called Grandmother, "come and see what I have made for you to take to Indiana." Grandmother stood in the doorway of the log cabin, and Susan was down near the brook. She was brushing aside the dead leaves and patches of snow, hunting for the first spring beauties. Though it was the middle of March, southern Kentucky lay warm in the spring sunshine, and Susan was without a hat.

Susan looked longingly at the brook as it

wound through a clump of willows. She was sure there would be spring beauties snuggled close to the old trees. But Grandmother stood waiting in the doorway, the sun glistening on her silvery hair.

Susan turned from the brook and ran up the hill toward the cabin. "Something to take with me to Indiana," she thought. What could it be? A quilt? A dress? Perhaps it was the old brass candlestick that Grandmother had promised Susan would be hers someday. Still it might be a new rag rug for Susan to put beside her bed to step onto on cold mornings. Susan knew Grandmother was always making rag carpets, when she wasn't knitting.

"Now shut your eyes and hold out your hands," laughed Grandmother, as she caught Susan in her arms, and placed her hands over her eyes.

Slowly she led Susan across the threshold of the cabin. "If we turn to the right, it will be a quilt, for Grandmother has put it on the bed," thought Susan. "If we go straight across the room, we will be walking toward the fireplace, and then I think it will be the candlestick that Grandmother keeps on the shelf above it. If we turn to the left, we will be near the old chest, and 'most anything could come out of that!"

Grandmother turned to the left, and stopped in front of the oak chest. “Keep your eyes closed tightly, Susan,” said Grandmother, “while I open the chest.”

“I will,” promised Susan, her eyes shut so tightly that her whole face was wrinkled. “But please hurry! I’m so curious I don’t believe I can wait another minute.”

Grandmother lifted out a long box smoothly covered with red calico. It was round, like a log, and in the middle was a leather strap sewed at both ends in Grandmother’s small even stitches to make a handle. She closed the chest and placed the long round box in Susan’s outstretched arms.

“Open your eyes now!” she said, laughing.

Susan opened her eyes. She looked at the bright red box wonderingly. Then she looked into her grandmother’s blue eyes.

“What is it, Grandmother? What is it?” she exclaimed. “Please tell me. I can’t wait to guess!”

“Sit down here, child,” was the answer. Grandmother pushed Susan’s own little stool with its woven cane seat toward her. “You can open the box by pulling out one end.”

Susan opened the box. “Oh, Grandmother, here’s a doll!” said she. “She’s dressed just like me. Her dress is made of the same calico mine is. Oh, you dear doll!" cried Susan, hugging the doll close in her arms. "She's so soft and cuddly. Her shoes and her sunbonnet are just like mine. Oh, Grandmother, thank you a hundred times."

She rushed to her grandmother and put one arm around her neck, holding the doll closely with the other. "I shall name her Abigail after you" she said earnestly.

"Thank you, dear. I'd like that," answered Grandmother. "The box she came in looks just like a traveling case I had when I was a little girl. It was called a portmanteau. So here is Abigail with her portmanteau, ready to leave for Indiana whenever you are. I meant to give her to you for Christmas," continued Grandmother, "but when I knew you all were going to Indiana this spring, I said to myself, 'Little Susan will grow tired on such a long journey, and I'll hurry and make that doll for her to play with on the way.' I've been planning for a long time to make her for you, so I set right to work. She's stuffed with wool from your grandfather's sheep, Susan, so when she gets dirty you can wash her. I made her jointed so she can sit down, too."

Grandmother set Abigail down carefully on

the floor beside Susan and looked affectionately at the two small figures, each so like the other.

"What a pretty face! Did you paint it, Grandmother?" asked Susan when she had taken the doll in her arms again, and was looking happily into its blue eyes.

"No, your Aunt Rachel did that," said Grandmother. "All last fall she gathered roots and berries and tried to find which dyes looked best. Then she began painting faces! She painted faces on her milk glass plate, then washed them off so she could try again. When she made one to suit her, she brought it over to show to me. I declare, I was as pleased when I saw it as you are now," laughed Grandmother.

"Uncle Mat made the box to carry her in. He never could think of the word portmanteau. He called it her satchel when he brought it over for me to cover and sew on the handle."

"It's all so very lovely," said Susan softly.

"You take good care of her and she will last all of your life, and then your little girl can have her to play with, for she's well sewed," exclaimed Grandmother proudly. "Now I must go and help your mother sort out the bedding. There's lots of work getting ready to move," she sighed as she hurried out of the door, leaving Susan alone with her doll.

The warm Kentucky sunshine poured in through the open door on Susan as she sat on her little stool with Abigail in her arms. Soon she took off Abigail's sunbonnet, and one sunbeam fell on the doll's face, lighting up her blue eyes.

"Oh, Abigail, I've always wanted a real doll! I love you so much, and I'll take good care of you always," whispered Susan. "I'm glad you can go on a journey with me to Brown County, Indiana, to our new home. We'll have lots of fun, won't we?"

Father, Mother, big brother David, and brother James did all they could for Susan Calvin; Timothy, the baby was fun, too, but Susan longed for a little girl to play with. Here was Abigail, with her portmanteau, ready to go to Indiana before Susan herself was ready to leave!

All the previous winter Father and Mother had talked of leaving their old home in Kentucky, and moving north to the new state of Indiana. Land was cheap there, and very rich, so Mr. Calvin had been told by the hunters and trappers who drifted through the new territory. David and James would soon be wanting to have farms of their own.

Father's brother, Uncle Sam, had taken his family north to Indiana many years earlier.

"Uncle Sam had moved his family to that part of Indiana known as the New Purchase soon after the Treaty of St. Marys had been signed with the Indians. According to this treaty, the Indians, for a sum of money, gave up all claim to the territory. The United States government opened it to the settlers, and Uncle Sam had been one of the first to secure rich farmlands there for his new home.

Though letters came seldom, Father knew Uncle Sam was well pleased with his new home. Susan thought of all this. Then she went to the shelf above the fireplace and took down a letter which was kept under the brass candlestick.

"I think, Abigail, I shall read you this letter," she said to her doll. "Father has read it to Mother so often through the long winter evenings that I almost know it by heart. Then you'll know where we're going, and why."

August 25, 1835

Dear Brother Tom:

Things are going well with us here in Brown County — good crops, and stock in fine shape. Why don't you come up next spring and join us? There are fine opportunities here. You can buy all the land you want — good bottom land it is, very rich soil — at two dollars an acre. I've a parcel of land in mind for you not far from us, up Bean Blossom way.

Last year we boiled down a good bit of salt from Salt Creek and sold it for $8.00 a bushel over in Bloomington. Jacob Nealy has just opened a tannery on Bean Blossom Creek and is doing right well with it. There's a fellow here by the name of Richards who has us all worked up about panning gold. I saw a phial filled with nuggets of gold and silver he told me he had panned in Lick Creek. I haven't been doing any panning myself, but I'm aiming to one of these days. Elijah Scarborough is building a flatboat and hopes to get to New Orleans with it in high water—from Salt Creek to the Driftwood River, to the Wabash into the Ohio, and then straight down the Mississippi.

Tell Carrie the hills are real pretty. There's talk of starting a school in Jacksonburg next fall, and there's a Baptist Church here now. Good healthy climate it is—almost no 'agur' this year.

We'll make room for you in our cabin while you're building yours. Better decide to come, Tom, you won't regret it. Tell

Susan her Cousin Samanthy wants to see her.

Your brother,
Sam

Susan's voice stopped. She put the letter back in its place under the brass candlestick, and she and Abigail sat together, very quietly.

Then she continued to the doll, "About Christmas time we decided to go, and now Grandmother and Grandfather have come to help us get started. He has loaned us his big canvas to cover the wagon, and he said he would put it on, too. Father and the boys have gathered together the farm things ready to pack into the wagon. Mother and Grandmother have been packing all week.

"I've told you all about our plans now, except we're supposed to finish packing in the morning. Let's go outside now, so you'll see something of Kentucky before you go travelling."

CHAPTER II
PLANNING THE JOURNEY

"Mother, see the new doll Grandmother made for me! Isn't she the loveliest doll you ever saw?" cried Susan a few minutes later as she ran to where Mother was hanging up Tim's freshly washed clothes.

"Let me see her, Susan. Grandmother told me about her, and I am anxious to see what she's like," said Mother, drying her hands and taking the doll. "Isn't her hair pretty! I do believe you can braid it, just as you do your own. And what a good size she is! Have you noticed that her dress buttons and unbuttons? I never knew anyone who could make as beautiful buttonholes as Grandmother, either. She has real little leather shoes that tie. Do you remember what a dreadful time you had learning to untie your shoes without making hard knots?"

Grandmother came toward them, and Mother turned to her as she said, "Rachel has certainly made a good face. Do you know she really looks a mite like Susan, doesn't she? She looks as though she could almost talk. You've dressed her just like Susan too, with pantalets, a sunbonnet, and a slate on her arm. What a lot of work you put on her, Mother! It will make the journey a much happier one for Susan when she has this doll to play with," said Mother with a smile. She handed Abigail to Susan, and continued hanging up the rest of the clothes.

"Don't call her 'the doll', Mother," said Susan. "She's Abigail. I've named her after Grandmother."

"All right, Susan, I think Abigail is a beautiful name. I wanted to name you Abigail, too, but your father wanted to call you Susan after his mother."

"Where are your father and Tom, Carrie?" asked Grandmother. Mother's name was Caroline, but Grandmother had always called her Carrie since Susan could remember.

"They've taken the boys and gone into the woods to cut saplings for the wagon top," answered Mother, hanging the last stocking on the line.

"Well, while we three women are here alone, isn't it a good time for us to go back to the cabin to gather together what you will want to take with you?" asked Grandmother.

Feeling quite grown up to be included as the third woman, Susan said, "We can't travel without eating. We will need the kettles, and pan, and the dishes, too." Grandmother and Mother exchanged glances of approval at Susan's practical suggestion.

"Tom and I have made a list of nearly everything we can take," said Mother, "and we sold a good many things along with the farm. Isn't it fine, Mother, we will have enough money to buy quite a piece of land in Indiana, and still have enough left to get a good start there."

"Yes, I'm mighty glad for you, Carrie. Has the man who bought your farm paid the money yet?" asked Grandmother anxiously.

"He gave Tom a hundred dollars last week. and has promised he will pay seventy-five dollars when he sells the stock in the fall. Then he will pay the other seventy-five dollars next year."

'That's fine! Yes, that's all right. Let me see, you are taking all the kettles and pans and dishes Susan spoke of. I'll put them all in this 'tater basket so you will have them in one place on the trip. We can put the food in one end of the basket, and the kettle, frying pan, and dishes in the other end."

The 'tater basket was a big willow basket, and Susan could never remember the time when it hadn't stood in the lean-to. She was glad it could go with them to Indiana.

Grandmother hummed a little song as she bustled about, gathering up the different things. She was happy to know that Carrie was going to a larger farm and richer land. Next year she and Grandfather would be there, too, for they had already promised that they would come to them in another year.

"I'll put only the things we will need on the journey in that basket," said Mother, "and we can put it under the wagon seat where we can get at it easily. Susan, put in the two brass kettles, the frying pan, the tin cups, the mush bowls we'll eat out of them, I guess—and the knives, forks, and wooden spoons. We will pack the big iron kettle, the pewter plates, the candle moulds, the chopping-bowl, and all our best things in a box."

"May I take my pewter mug, the one you used when you were a little girl, Mother?" interrupted Susan.

"Yes, of course! The boys will be driving the cows north, too, and you can drink your milk from it just as you always do. But we aren't going to be able to take all of our furniture. Tom says there won't be room in the wagon. We will have to take the bureau, and I must take the chest Father made for me before I was married, and—would you take the cradle, Mother?"

"Yes, I would. You rocked all your babies in that cradle, and you just ought to keep it for your grandchildren; squeeze it in some place."

"Mother," spoke up Susan, "you must take your rocking chair. It wouldn't seem like home unless you sat mending and rocking in front of the fire. I want to rock Abigail in it sometimes, too," she urged.

"Susan, when we come up next year I'll get Grandfather to make you a little hickory rocking chair for Abigail. Carrie, be sure to take your cherry candlestand; your Father made that down in Virginia, and it is the most beautiful thing you have."

"Yes, and the hickory chairs, and Susan's stool. Oh! There's the baby crying. Will you and Susan look over the garden seeds? Be sure to get all of them," she called over her shoulder, as she hurried away to care for Timothy.

"I haven't my spectacles here, Susan; you read me the names of the seeds your mother has on this list and I will put them in the seed basket."

Susan read slowly, for Mother's writing was hard to read: "Beans, cabbage, sweet corn, beets, onions, carrots, turnips, tobacco—"

"Wait a minute," interrupted Grandmother, "I can't find the tobacco seed. There must be more seeds somewhere! Look on the top cupboard shelf, Susan, I believe I saw some there the other day."

Susan brought a chair, climbed up, and by standing on her tiptoes was able to reach the top shelf. "Yes, here are more seeds in this jar; will you take them so I won't spill them?"

"Yes, this is the tobacco seed," nodded Grandmother. "Now go on reading the list."

"—Sorghum, popcorn, sunflower, hollyhock, bleeding heart, petunia, cockscomb, mignonette.

But aren't we going to take any wheat or barley, or 'taters, or cattle corn?" asked Susan.

"I'm sure your Father and the boys will take care of all those. I remember seeing a sack of corn and clover seed in the barn this morning, and a basket of sweet 'taters, too."

"I hope Mother takes the clock. I like to sit by the fire at night and make up stories about the picture on the face of the clock of the little girl and boy going up the road to a white church."

"You must remember, Susan, that you can't get everything you want into one covered wagon! It won't hold much. Your father and mother will only be able to take the most necessary things. But I do think your mother should take her clock. You can't buy a Seth Thomas clock every day, and that one keeps good time."

All through that spring afternoon Susan and Grandmother worked together, even while Mother prepared supper. In fact Grandfather, Father, David, and James found them still working when Mother called them to come in for the meal.

When supper was over and the dishes washed, Susan drew her little three-legged stool close to Grandmother's knee. Grandmother was sitting before the open fireplace, finishing the knitting of a pair of socks for Father. Susan never tired of watching the needles flashing back and forth in the firelight. They seemed to fly, so fast did Grandmother knit. Susan, herself, could knit socks—she had knitted a pair for David last winter—but she knit very, very slowly and watched every stitch carefully, not like Grandmother who never looked at her knitting, even when she turned the heels and toes.

Without looking up from the harness he was mending, Grandfather asked, "Tom, how are you planning your trip?"

"Well, as near as I can reckon," Father replied, "it will take five days of good hard driving to get as far north as the Ohio River, and about a week longer to drive from there to Brown County. Sam writes that the last forty miles are bad roads, and we'll have to drive mighty slow. It's hilly when you get near Jacksonburg. James will ride Dan, and David will drive the cows. Enoch Wetzel just finished two fine yokes for the oxen."

"I've never seen finer oxen than yours," Grandfather remarked.

"That's about right! There are none better in all of Kentucky. They'll get us there safe and sound."

"David, are you going to leave Steve with me?" questioned Grandfather as he winked at Father. The family all knew that David wouldn't go a foot without his faithful hunting dog, Steve.

"Not by a jug full, I'm not," laughed Dave goodnaturedly. "He'll make the trip all right. Won't you, old dog?" asked David, patting the dog's head. Steve seemed to understand, and wagged his tail agreeably.

"How about chickens? Are you going to take any?" asked James.

"Oh, yes, you must take enough to start a new flock. Have you cooked any to eat on the way, Carrie?" asked Grandmother.

"Yes, I've roasted four; and Rachel brought over a black walnut cake for us to eat on our first Sunday. With what game the men will kill, salt pork, and the corncakes I'll stir up, we'll get along beautifully," Mother replied.

"We'll swing the chicken coop under the wagon."

"It will travel all right, won't it, Grandfather?" questioned Father.

"Sure enough! Sure enough!" was the answer. "I brought a coop full from Virginia with us that way, when we came up."

"I think we have everything ready to load," Father said slowly as if thinking aloud: "Scythe, grindstone, shovel, spade, pickax, crowbar, hoe, rake, crane, axes, broadax, plough. Did I leave anything out?" he asked.

"Don't forget your carpenter tools, you'll need them," reminded Grandfather.

"That's right! Of course! It's funny how you forget things, isn't it?"

"Did you look at the sky tonight, Father?" asked Mother anxiously. "We could never pack the wagon in the rain. Oh, I do hope we have a good day to start. Susan Calvin!" exclaimed Mother, "it's long past your bedtime, and tomorrow will be such a busy day. Hurry to bed."

"Carrie, this is the last night I'll have the child with me. Let me tell her just one little story," urged Grandmother. "Come, Susan, climb up in my lap and I'll tell you a story about a lazy boy who grew to be one of Virginia's finest men, and one of America's great leaders."

"Goody! Goody! Grandmother, may Abigail come, too?"

"Of course she may, if you'll promise to hurry to bed quickly after I finish."

The firelight played on the intent faces of

Susan and Abigail as they both sat in Grandmother's lap.

CHAPTER III
GRANDMOTHER'S STORY

I'm going to tell you tonight about a man whom all Virginians are proud to call their own—Patrick Henry. He was one of my dear father's closest friends, and he often came to our home to spend the night. I've heard my father tell of what a lazy boy Patrick was. He wouldn't work at anything! He wouldn't study, and he didn't seem to learn much of anything at school. He loved to play on his flute and his fiddle, and to gather a group of people around Hanover Court House and tell them funny stories.

"His father thought that if he had his own business he might then start to work, so he started him and his older brother into business. But that had no effect on Patrick, and soon the business failed. Then Patrick went to farming and failed. He went back to storekeeping and failed. People felt sorry for Patrick's father, but Patrick himself didn't seem to worry. He had a good time playing for dances and telling his amusing stories.

"For some reason, my father never knew why, Patrick Henry decided to study law. Perhaps he could work with his mind better than with his hands. He began to read law books; he read diligently for six weeks, and to everyone's surprise, he passed the examination and was admitted to the bar."

"Clients began to come to him. He was pleasant and jolly, and people liked him. Most important of all, Patrick liked law work, and kept at it. His friends were still more surprised when he offered to take a case for some of the people of Virginia against the parsons."

"You see we often did not have money to pay our parsons or ministers, so we paid them in tobacco. You know, Susan, tobacco is a chief crop of Virginia. Sometimes tobacco would be worth a great deal of money and then the parsons would feel well paid. Other times tobacco wouldn't be worth much, so the parsons wouldn't get much pay."

"Finally they asked to be paid only in money, and a law was passed which made it necessary for the people to pay the parsons in money. Then a queer thing happened—tobacco went away up in value—and the parsons were cross because they were paid in money; if payment had been made with tobacco they would have had three times as much money. So one of the parsons brought suit to get more money! King George heard of this, inquired about the law, and said it was not right. The citizens who felt the law was right then asked Patrick Henry to speak for them."

"My father was one of the men who asked Patrick Henry to defend them. He often told us how frightened he felt when Patrick stood up to talk. He said he never felt so sorry for any man! Patrick couldn't seem to talk; he stumbled and halted in a dreadful fashion."

"Then suddenly he changed. He stood up very straight; his manner became dignified; his voice grew strong; his eyes flashed. Father said his words rushed forth like a mighty torrent. Such eloquence had never before been heard in the

Virginia colony. His courage astounded his hearers, for he told the colonists that King George had no right to say that laws which the Virginia legislature had passed were not right. Thus, he questioned the right of the King—something which had never been done before."

"And what do you think, Susan! The jury decided that the colonists were right. Patrick Henry had won his case, which was called the 'Parson's Cause.' "

"From then on success came rapidly to Patrick. He had found what he liked to do. In two years he was a member of the legislature. My father said that Patrick Henry's words were the first words of the American Revolution. No man ever felt the same after he had heard them. We didn't have war for ten years, but this was the first time the colonies had differed from the mother country."

"With all Patrick's careless habits, he was a man of high honor and integrity. He began to improve his manners and his way of talking. He was soon changed into a new man—one of culture, learning, and extraordinary powers of oratory. He was often called 'the silver-tongued orator."

"He was sent to Philadelphia as a member of the First Continental Congress. Father also heard him speak before the House of Burgesses. He said he had never heard such a burst of eloquence. Patrick Henry told of the tyranny of the King and declared there was nothing to do but fight! Father said people will always remember that speech—it will go down in American history—never to be forgotten. Some day, Susan, you will learn all of that speech by heart. He closed by saying, 'I know not what course others may take; but as for me, give me liberty or give me death.'

"How different from the lazy, idle boy was this man who could arouse his listeners with his fine thoughts and his wonderful oratory. In time he was elected governor of Virginia. I want you always to remember Patrick Henry, Susan. He was one of the finest of Virginia's sons, and one of the great men of America."

"Now run along to bed!"

Susan, with Abigail in her arms, slipped down from Grandmother's lap. 'That was a lovely story," she whispered. "I'll always remember it, and I'll tell it to Abigail again and again, so she won't forget it, either!"

She kissed Grandmother and Grandfather, and called good night to the others. Mother handed her a lighted candle, and away she went with Abigail to the back room. She pulled out her trundle bed from under Mother's big bed. When she lifted up the pillow to get her nightgown and nightcap, she found lying underneath, a second nightgown and nightcap just like her own, but very small. Pinned to them was a slip of paper, and written on it in Grandmother's small, fine writing were the words: *For Abigail.*

"Oh, Abigail, here are your own nightgown and nightcap," explained Susan to Abigail. "As soon as we put them on, you can sleep here with me in my bed. Isn't that fun? You're very warm and soft—not like the wooden doll Uncle Mat carved for me!"

In a few moments Susan blew out the candle. There was a deep stillness in the room for several moments as she knelt by the side of her trundle bed.

Then she climbed in, and pulled the patchwork quilt up closely about them both, saying softly to the doll, "I've just said my prayers, Abigail. Mother taught them to me when I was a very small girl, almost as soon as I could talk. I don't believe the prayers I say would be the ones for me to teach you, though." Susan thought a moment. "I know! I'll teach you my favorite poem. Grandmother taught it to me, and she said she thought it was as lovely as a prayer of thanksgiving."

WE THANK THEE .

For flowers that bloom about our feet;
For tender grass so fresh, so sweet;
For song of bird, and hum of bee;
For all things fair we hear or see;
Father in heaven, we thank Thee!

For blue of stream and blue of sky;
For pleasant shades of branches high;
For fragrant air and cooling breeze;
For beauty of the blooming trees;
Father in heaven, we thank thee!
—Anonymous

When Susan went to sleep, Abigail was close in her arms, and Abigail's portmanteau, tightly shut, was on the floor close beside the trundle bed.

"Here are your own nightgown and nightcap"

CHAPTER IV
OFF FOR INDIANA

Mother's hope was fulfilled. The next moming was bright and clear, a perfect day to start on the journey.

"Up, everybody!" called Father. "Get up, lazybones. Today we leave for Brown County. Everybody up!"

Susan hopped out of bed and looked out of the window as she was dressing, so as to watch the men bending and fitting the long bows over the top of the wagon. Great high hoops they seemed to be which made a framework over which the large white canvas would soon be stretched. Grandfather's careful work in cutting and shaping the bows, and his painstaking efforts of the past few days resulted in each hoop bending and fitting into place without difficulty.

"There, now, that's good and firm, and will hold," she heard Grandfather say proudly, as he slipped the last bow in place. Next, the canvas was thrown over the bows, stretched tightly, and tied down securely.

"When your Grandmother and I used that canvas coming up from Virginia years ago, we never supposed our little Caroline would be using it to go up to Indiana," said Grandfather to Susan and Abigail who had run out and stood beside him. "It's as fine and heavy a piece as I ever saw; no water can get through that."

Grandfather stood back and proudly surveyed his work. Instead of the old wagon that Susan had seen so often, there stood a real covered wagon, just the kind she had seen some of their old friends start away in.

"Let me pull up the cord in front," pleaded Susan, running up to the wagon. Tall, slender David swung her up in his strong arms, and showed her how to draw the heavy cord so as to gather the canvas across the front end of the wagon. When the canvas was in place, he tied the cord for her in a hard knot.

"You see, Susan, we make the first bow stick out over the seat to keep out the sun and rain," David told her. Then Susan realized that it was really a roof over the wagon seat.

"It looks mighty fine now, doesn't it?" asked James who had been working inside the wagon. Almost as tall as David, perhaps even more tanned, he managed to crowd a good time for Susan into all he did. "Climb over the seat, Susan, and see the inside of your house where you will live for two weeks."

"It makes a fine little cabin, doesn't it?" said Susan, jumping up and down with delight, when James had set her safely down.

"Get down now, Susan," said Father, "We've got to load. Come on, boys. Dave, you take one end of this chest and I'll take the other. After we get it in the wagon, you shove it back in place, James."

"Father, we'll have to take out the drawers. Mother has packed them so full we can never lift the chest with them in," answered David.

With the three men pushing and lifting, up into the wagon went the bureau. David and James quickly put the drawers back in place. Next came the chairs, and next, Tim's cradle. As she watched, Susan realized that Father was finding room for everything—all garden tools, and even the basket of seeds. The feather beds were piled in last to make a comfortable seat for Susan and Abigail.

"Come, everybody," called Mother, "and we'll have our last breakfast at the old house. Then we'll hitch the oxen and start."

The cabin seemed queer with no furniture in it, and no place to sit, so they decided to eat in front of the cabin in the early spring sunshine.

Grandfather looked around at the family with their steaming bowls of food in their hands. Mother with baby Tim in her arms, sat on the cabin step. Father, tall and slender, with a heavy beard that was fast turning gray, stood near her. Grandmother was helping happy, ten-year old Susan to a second bowl of mush. David and James, tall and tanned, sat crosslegged on the grass, with Steve not far away. Abigail sat leaning against a tree with her sunbonnet in her lap. Grandfather looked at the group, slowly cleared his throat, and said solemnly, "Folks, you are starting on a long journey. It is good to ask the Lord's blessing on you."

Lowering his voice he continued: "Lord, these, my folks, are leaving us to take a hard journey. They need strength. Give it to them. They need health.

Give it to them. Keep them good men and women. Keep them honest, and make them good neighbors. Lord, keep them with you, and they will help to make the new land a good land. Amen."

For several moments not a word was spoken. Father and Mother, Grandfather and Grandmother looked very serious as they gazed off across the hills of Kentucky. The older boys squared their shoulders, and Susan, herself, felt the importance of leaving an old home and going to a new one as she had not felt it before.

Soon the simple breakfast was eaten, the dishes washed and packed away under the seat, and they were ready to leave. "If you are ready, Carrie," called Grandfather, "you can all drive by way of our place, and we'll take Susan with us in the buggy."

"You won't have a buggy to ride in up in Brown County, Susan." Said Grandmother as Grandfather lifted her up to the seat between them, and handed her Abigail with her portmanteau.

The winding road led down one hill and up another. Never had the trees looked prettier than they did this early morning in the spring sunshine.

"I'm very glad Abigail will have such a pretty picture of Kentucky to remember," said Susan seriously as she took deep breaths of the soft, spring air.

Soon they reached Grandfather's and Grandmother's home, for it was only a mile away. Aunt Rachel and Uncle Mat sat on the porch waiting for them, as they had driven over to say good-by.

"Oh, Aunt Rachel, thank you for making Abigail such a sweet face,“ cried Susan, rushing up to her favorite aunt the moment Uncle Mat had lifted her down from the buggy.

"I tried to make her look like you," laughed Aunt Rachel as she patted Susan's rosy cheek. Then they both turned to wave to Father and Mother, who were sitting on the high seat of the covered wagon just turning into the yard.

All too soon, greetings changed to good-bys, as Father finally called, "Come, come, we must get started!"

"Good-by, Grandmother, you'll surely join us next spring, won't you?" asked Mother as she hugged Grandmother close. "We'll be looking for you too, Rachel and Mat," she added, kissing them, and climbing up on the seat.

"Yes, we'll be coming up sure," answered Grandmother as she kissed baby Tim good by, and lifted him up to his mother. "Come, Susan, you're next!"

"Oh, Grandmother and Grandfather, I can't

leave you! I can't!" said Susan, bursting into tears and flinging her arms around Grandmother's neck. "Please let me stay here with you, please. I'll be ever so good. I don't want to go to that new place, truly I don't."

"There now, Susan child, this is no way for a pioneer girl to act. I'm ashamed of you, I am," said Grandmother. "It isn't as though you were going way off by yourself—you're going with the family, aren't you? Don't let your mother see you cry! And what will Abigail think!"

Susan was so busy wiping her eyes and blowing her nose that she didn't notice the tears in Grandmother's eyes, nor did she see Grandfather blowing his nose the other side of the wagon, or Mother in the front seat silently crying. Going away wasn't fun after all! How could she have ever thought it would be? But when Grandfather lifted her up onto the feather bed in the back of the wagon, she managed a little smile through her tears.

"My brave girl," said he, giving her a hug as he settled her comfortably beside Abigail on the blanket Mother had laid over the feather bed.

"Now you, James, keep an eye on your little sister," cautioned Grandfather as James came striding up, a long switch in his hand.

"Sure, I'll watch her all right," he said gaily.

Uncle Mat and Aunt Rachel kissed Susan, and they shook hands with Abigail, wishing her a pleasant journey. Soon all were in their places. Dave, with Steve close beside him, was riding Dan, the horse, ready to help James with the cows whenever he was needed. Mother was sitting on the front seat holding Tim. Father stood by the oxen with his long whip in his hand.

"Ged-dap," shouted Father in a sharp, ringing voice as he cracked his whip over the oxen. The covered wagon began to move, and they were off on their long journey.

"Good-by, good by," each was calling to the other above the creaking of the wagon wheels. Susan waved her handkerchief as long as she could see Grandmother standing before the cabin door, waving her apron.

"Oh, Abigail, I am so glad you are here with me," whispered Susan as she settled herself on the feather bed, ready for a good long cry.

Perhaps she imagined it; perhaps it was Grandmother's loving encouragement ringing in her ears; but she was sure she heard Abigail say, "Susie, I'm disappointed in you. I thought you were a brave girl, and I've been proud to belong to you. But I'm beginning to believe you're just a baby. You'll make me cry in a minute, and I haven't anything to cry about! I'm with you, and you are the only person I love. Stop crying and behave yourself. This is a great adventure for me, Susan, for I've never gone traveling and you'll have to explain many things to me."

"I suppose you are right," Susan heard herself say as she settled herself deeper in the feather bed and straightened Abigail's bonnet. "But I'm very sorry to leave Grandfather and Grandmother."

Father drove the yoke of oxen drawing the covered wagon down the hill and followed the winding road to the little village Susan knew so well. It was fun to wave good-by to their different friends who gathered outside the cabin doors as they passed.

"Good luck to ye! Hope you like the new country," called Hiram Green.

"Good luck!" called Andy Taggart.

"Send us back word if the new land is better'n ourn," shouted Enoch Wetzel.

"Mayhap we'll be moving up next spring," called Joshua Prentiss.

Each family had some greeting for them as they passed. Susan called and waved in return to everybody as they went along. When they passed the Kennedy cabin, Susan's best friend, Nancy Kennedy, ran out and tossed a package in the wagon as she said good-by.

"Oh! Thank you, thank you!" called Susan.

When she picked up the package to open it she saw printed on the outside of it the words: *Do not open this until the day after you reach your new home.*

"My!" thought Susan. "I can have such fun guessing what is in it. It seems to be round and fairly large. It's not very soft and not very hard. Maybe it's a ball, or perhaps a pin cushion." Susan felt of it again carefully. Then she exclaimed, "I think it's a basket, for Nancy makes the loveliest willow baskets! I believe this one has a handle. Wasn't that sweet of her. Oh, Abigail, you will like my friends," she said, turning to the doll. "My friends are very nice. I 'most forgot! I won't have any friends up in Indiana! What will I do?" said Susan, partly to her self and partly to Abigail.

Without waiting for an answer, she continued, "But there are little girls everywhere, aren't there, Abigail? I guess most of them are nice, too, if you're nice to them. I'll have good friends in Indiana if I had good friends in Kentucky, won't I?"

The wagon lurched as the road turned sharply, and Abigail in her sunbonnet seemed to nod her head emphatically in complete agreement.

the meal started first." Then she ran off with the basket in which the tin cups jingled gaily.

"Look out, boys, not too big a fire!" cautioned Father, as he looked back from unyoking the oxen.

"Mother, this yoke is fine. We've been traveling for at least nine miles, and there isn't a chafing mark on the animals."

"I think an ox yoke is the most clumsy looking thing I've ever seen," remarked Mother. "At this rate we ought to be there in a week, don't you think, Tom?"

"Oh, we won't have good roads like this all the way. Dave, drive the cattle down to the creek for a good drink."

With the places set and the food unpacked, Susan ran back to the wagon, picked up Abigail, and brought her over to the fire where they could both watch Mother preparing the meal. Potatoes with their jackets on were boiling in the big black kettle over the fire, and a pot of coffee was steaming at one side.

"Dave, give the oxen and the horses their grain, and then we'll wash up for dinner," said Father, as Mother came back from the wagon with Tim in her arms. Laying him on a blanket under a tree, she took Susan's hand and they walked down to the spring.

"Isn't it fun traveling in a covered wagon and eating outdoors, Mother? I just love it, especially now that I have Abigail to share things with me." And Susan talked on, telling her Mother of her plans for Abigail. "She needs a cloak the first thing, or a plaid shawl. I'm surprised Grandmother let her start on such a long journey without one."

Susan noticed that Mother smiled queerly when she spoke of a coat, and the next day Susan understood what that queer smile meant.

"Here is Grandmother's lunch basket. Let's see what's in it," said Father, bringing from under the seat of the wagon a large green willow basket. "I smell fried chicken," he said, as he untied the cloth that covered the basket top.

Father picked up a large piece of paper from the top of the basket and read aloud in an amused voice, "Eat only what you find on the top layer today."

"Well, what if that isn't enough?" asked David.

"Oh, let me see what Grandmother made for us!" exclaimed Mother eagerly. Mother had never outgrown her love of surprises, and Grandmother had kept the contents of the basket a complete surprise. "Oh, Susan, did you ever see such beautiful fried chicken! Grandmother must have gotten up before daylight to get it fried," said Mother, as she joyfully held up a tin plate heaped high with golden brown pieces. "And here's a jar of her pickled onions—Father's favorite! Here's a dried apple pie. What's this?" Then she picked up a package. Across the top of it was written in Grandmother's fine writing: *For Carrie from Grandmother, for her new home.*

Opening the package she found one of Grandmother's rare old treasures—a lovely milk glass plate.

"How good of Grandmother! She knows how much I have always admired that plate," said Mother. Her eyes filled with tears as she thought of her mother's generosity.

"Come to the feast, boys," briskly called Father. How they all did enjoy their food, and how they did laugh at baby Tim putting his toes in his mouth, instead of the chicken bone Mother gave him.

When the meal was finished the dishes were washed and repacked, and again Susan and Abigail found themselves comfortably settled on the feather bed in the covered wagon.

The oxen moved slowly down the winding Kentucky road. The ground was dry and firm and the wagon wheels rolled easily in the well packed ruts. The covered wagon seemed to sway to the slow plodding gait of the oxen, and in a few moments Susan fell asleep.

Late in the afternoon Susan was awakened by Mother's voice calling, "Wake up! Wake up! We're stopping for supper and to make camp. What a sleepyhead you are. Riding in a wagon makes you sleep a long time, doesn't it?"

"Where am I?" asked Susan, sitting up and rubbing her eyes.

"You are in a covered wagon," laughed Mother, "somewhere in northern Kentucky, on your way to the hills of Brown County in Indiana. Come and watch baby Tim while I walk around to limber up. I'm very stiff from sitting so long."

Susan climbed down out of the wagon as Mother lay the baby on the blanket on the ground and began walking briskly.

"Where's Dave?" called Father. Everybody looked back down the road, but no Dave and no cows were in sight.

"I hope nothing has happened to him," said Mother anxiously.

"It's a slow job driving those cows along," said James, riding up. "They're probably slower this afternoon because they are all tuckered out. If he doesn't come along soon, I'll ride back."

"I'll go back now and let him ride Dan in," said Father, jumping on Dan's back and galloping away.

They all lay down on the blanket under the trees to rest and to watch baby Tim, who was cooing and gurgling softly.

"Tim seems to like traveling in a covered wagon, doesn't he, Mother?" asked Susan. "Isn't it lucky he is such a good baby? It would be too bad if he were like the Taggert baby who cried all the time."

"That would certainly make it much harder," agreed Mother.

In a very short time David came trotting up on Dan.

"What happened, Dave?" shouted James.

Mother inquired anxiously, "Are you all right?"

"Oh, sure! I'm all right, but those tarnal cows want to stop and eat all the time. It's a job keeping them on the move," exploded David.

"Gentle, gentle," said Mother quietly.

"You wouldn't be gentle if you had to drive them, Mother. I can hear myself saying much worse things about them than that by tomorrow evening."

At that moment Father came up with the

cattle. "That's a tiresome job, all right. I think I'll have to drive the cows each afternoon and have the boys take their turns mornings. Drive the animals down to the spring, boys, and bring back a bucket of water. This is rather wild country and there should be good game about. James, I suppose you are too tired to go hunting, aren't you?" queried Father, with a jovial smile.

The weary James immediately changed to an eager, lively boy as he grinned and said, "Come on and get the guns! Let's go! We might see a turkey. If we do, that would be the end of Mr. Gobbler!"

As soon as the cattle were watered and grazing, the three men left with their guns to look for game. They followed a winding footpath that was soon lost in the very dense woods.

Halfway across the clearing David turned and ran back saying, "Here's a gun, Mother. Father said it would be safer for you to have one with you in this unsettled, wooded country. I'll lean it here against the tree for you. But remember! It's loaded."

With a cheery smile he was gone.

"Why, Mother, can you shoot a gun?" asked Susan in a surprised voice.

"Not very well, Susan. I have done it, of

course, but not often. I suppose I could if it were necessary, though," she added, as much to herself as to Susan.

CHAPTER VI
THE BEAR

The sun was setting and the tall trees cast heavy shadows across the grass. The spring and the brook which led from it made strange noises as the water bubbled up, and rushed against the banks. The wind rustled through the trees, and deep in the woods a whippoorwill called. Susan watched a squirrel scurry to its nest hidden among the leaves of the tallest tree near the clearing.

Unconsciously, Mother and Susan were talking in low tones. Tim was asleep, and Abigail sat not far away, leaning against a tree.

Suddenly Susan heard a rustling in the bushes at the edge of the clearing behind Mother. A sharp *plop,* like the sound of a breaking log, split the stillness. Susan glanced over in that direction expecting to see Steve run toward them. But her little figure grew tense, her face frightened. She opened her mouth to speak, but no words came. Then she pointed a shaking hand beyond Mother's shoulder and whispered, "Mother, it's a bear!"

"Oh, it can't be, Susan, don't be imagining things!" Mother calmly answered before she turned about to look in the direction Susan pointed.

Then she glanced over her shoulder. There was a huge black bear, standing perfectly still with his head on one side looking at them. Mother felt herself grow rigid with fear. In the deep silence she could hear her own heart beat. The thought that Father and the boys were far in the woods, that the bear was coming closer, and that here were Susan and Tim to be taken care of, rushed through her mind. But she calmly said, "Sit perfectly still, Susan. Don't move an inch. I'll shoot him."

"How can Mother be so calm?" Susan thought, but as she watched, she saw how her mother's hands were shaking.

"What *can* I do to help?" the little girl

wondered. Then she remembered the old song Grandmother often sang whenever anything seemed very, very serious—*Take It to the Lord in Prayer.* Susan shut her eyes quickly. "Oh, dear Jesus," she whispered, "don't let the bear eat us. Help Mother to kill him. Amen."

Susan's eyes flew open. The bear was lumbering slowly across the clearing toward them. "Why doesn't Mother shoot! Why is she so slow! Oh, dear! Oh, dear!" thought Susan.

Seconds seemed hours to Susan as she watched Mother reach for the gun, reach so slowly that the bear did not seem to notice her movements. Mother braced it against the tree where it had been leaning. When the aim was true, and the gun was steady, Mother fired. The shot echoed and reechoed.

As the smoke cleared, Mother and Susan saw the bear lumbering away, back into the forest. In a moment Father came running up. "What is it? What is it?" he shouted. "Why did you shoot?"

"A bear." answered Mother excitedly.

"Oh, no, it couldn't have been! You must have been frightened," said Father.

David and James rushed up, David with a wild turkey slung over his shoulder and James with two squirrels on his belt.

"What's wrong? Who shot?" asked David.

"Mother thought she saw a bear," said Father.

"Tom, I did see a bear—a great big black bear. I think I wounded him when I shot. Take your gun and follow his trail back of that sycamore," said Mother, pointing to the big tree in front of which she had first seen the bear.

Father looked serious, and telling James to stay with Mother and Susan, he said, "Come, Dave, we'll see if we can find him."

Both men took their guns and hurried off into the woods.

"Mother, where's Abigail?" asked Susan.

"Here she is, dear," said Mother, putting Abigail in Susan's arms. "I really believe she fell over in fright when she saw the bear coming toward her."

"Or when she heard the gun," suggested James. "Did you kill the bear, Mother?" he continued. "Tell me all about it."

"I don't think I killed him, son. I'm pretty sure that I hit him, though."

"Did you get scared, Susan?" he asked his sister. "Was the bear a big one?"

"Well, I guess you'd be scared to see a great big black bear coming toward you!" answered Susan.

"James, the men will be hungry when they get back. Will you start a good fire, please?" asked

"She watched Mother reach for the gun"

practical Mother. "Susan, you—"

Bang! Bang! The report of a gun sounded twice.

"They've got him! They've got him!" shouted James, jumping up and down. "Can't I go, Mother?"

"Yes, run along, but leave a gun with me," was Mother's answer. "I've shot one bear today. I could shoot another, I guess."

Before long they heard the voices of the men returning through the woods. As soon as they reached Mother, the three men took hold of hands and formed a circle around Mother, singing:

Mother killed a bear,
Mother killed a bear,
Heigh o! the derry oh,
Mother killed a bear.

Susan laughed to see Father dancing and singing with the boys in such a funny way.

"You're a fine shot, Mother!" said Father. "You hit the bear near the heart. It ran only a few yards into the woods. Talk about beginner's luck! I couldn't have done better myself," and Father beamed with pride at his wife.

"Come and see your bear, Mother," cried David, swinging Susan up on his shoulder while James picked up Tim. Father took Mother's arm and led the procession back in the woods to the dead bear.

"Oh, let me down quick so I can see!" cried Susan, as David pointed to a big, black object lying under a tree.

"Did I really kill that big thing?" asked Mother doubtfully, as she gazed down at the bear. "Why did you shoot again, if I killed it?"

"We found him howling with rage and pain, so Dave and I each took a shot to finish him," explained Father.

"I claim the skin for a rug for the hearth of the fireplace in our new cabin," said Mother. "But, Susan, perhaps you should have it, for I think you saved my life because you warned me! You saw the bear first."

"Well, it isn't quite that bad," smiled Father. "If a bear is left alone, he doesn't often bother people. He probably smelled food, and came to get it. He might have attacked you, though, if you hadn't shot."

Susan began to tell how she looked up and saw the bear. Mother began to tell how she was so frightened that she could hardly hold the gun. David began to tell how lucky it was that he ran back with the gun and left it leaning against a tree that was within Mother's reach. It seemed as though they would never tire of talking about the bear.

In fact the time Mother shot the bear proved to be a favorite topic of conversation for many years in the Calvin family.

CHAPTER VII
MOTHER'S FAVORITE HYMN

Father and David decided they would stay to skin the bear. "We will have to salt it and roll up the skin until we have time to stretch it for drying," said Father. "Mother shall have her rug, and we'll take the choice parts of the meat with us."

Mother, James and Susan went back to prepare supper.

"Put some potatoes in the ashes to bake, James," suggested Mother. "We will have cold roast chicken, potatoes, milk and a surprise! We can't have the surprise without the hoe. Susan, while I milk Buttercup and Molly, you run over to the wagon and bring me the hoe. After you put the potatoes in to bake, James, take a bucket and bring some water from the spring."

Mother sat down to milk the cows as she finished speaking, and soon her pail was full of rich, foamy milk.

She poured some of the water James brought into one of the kettles hanging over the fire. When it began to boil, she stirred in some salt and corn meal. While she continued to stir it, she told James to take the handle off the hoe. Then she asked him to run back to Father to get some bear grease.

To Susan's surprise, she saw Mother clean off the hoe. When James returned, she greased it with bear grease, put the soft dough from the kettle on the hoe, and placed it near the fire. She answered the surprised expression on Susan's face by explaining, "This is going to be hoecake, but it will taste just like the johnnycake we used to make in Virginia. I know how to make it yet another way, too. Some day I'll wrap the dough up in cabbage leaves or in fresh corn husks and put it on the hearth and cover it with hot coals. We call that ashcake. You can do lots of things when you have to. In the new country we'll have to think of new ways to do a great many things, I imagine."

Everyone was ready for bed as soon as the supper things were all washed and carefully put away. No matter how tired she was, Mother insisted on all the work being done, and done well.

David built a blazing fire near the rear of the wagon and ordered Steve to stand guard. After gathering wood for the night, the three men rolled up in their blankets and lay down between the fire and the wagon with their guns close beside them. Mother, Timothy, Susan, and Abigail were safe and comfortable on the feather beds inside the wagon. The wind blew in sharp gusts about the covered wagon, but the canvas top held firm. Strange noises of the night drifted across the clearing from the woods beyond.

Susan lay wide awake with Abigail beside her. She heard Mother sigh—as though her thoughts were far from happy ones. Then Susan heard Father say something to the boys in a low undertone.

All was still—as though the whole woods stood silent to listen. Then Father's voice began to sing Mother's favorite hymn. David's ringing baritone took up the tune, and in a moment James joined the singing.

At the end of the first verse Susan began to sing, too, and before the third verse was finished, Mother found herself singing in the clear soprano all her children loved.

AWAKE MY SOUL, STRETCH EVERY NERVE

Awake, my soul, stretch every nerve,
And press with vigor on;
A heav'nly race demands thy zeal,
And an immortal crown.

A cloud of witnesses around
Hold thee in full survey;
Forget the steps already trod,
And onward urge thy way.

'Tis God's all animating voice
That calls thee from on high;
'Tis His own hand presents the prize
To thine aspiring eye.

That prize with peerless glories bright
Which shall new luster boast,
When victors wreaths and monarchs gems
Shall blend in common dust.

Blest Savior, introduced by Thee,
Have I my race begun;
And, crowned with vict'ry, at Thy feet
I'll lay my honors down.

Each one of the five verses rang clear and true through the Kentucky wilderness. But as the words of the last verse ended, the very wind seemed more friendly, its harsh gusts changing to a gentle, drowsy lullaby.

In a few moments the Calvins were asleep.

* * * * *

The next morning Mother handed Susan a package from Grandmother as she said, "You see, Susan, Grandmother has another surprise for you."

When Susan opened the package, she found a piece of cloth cut from an old plaid shawl which she had seen Grandmother wear many, many times. A sheet of paper was fastened to it with one of the largest pins Susan had ever seen. She read the paper: *Dear Susan: Use this big pin to ravel out the cloth around each edge to make a fringe for a shawl for Abigail.*

To Susan's surprise, under the package which contained the material for Abigail's shawl was a second square package. In it she found a piece of brown cloth which she recognized as a piece left from the cloth Grandmother, herself, had woven for her warm winter coat. In the same package were a pattern for both a coat and a bonnet, and thread and needles.

In a tiny box was a little silver thimble with a name engraved on it.

Susan looked at the thimble carefully, and spelled out each letter of the name aloud, "T-h-u-r-z-a. Why, that must have belonged to Grandmother's mother," said Susan. "Grandmother's name is Abigail, and her mother's name was Thurza. Grandmother told me all about her! She must have had that thimble when she was a little girl in Virginia."

Folded in this package was a long letter in Grandmother's fine, small writing. It read:

> Dear Susan:
>
> Here is some cloth for a coat and a bonnet for Abigail. If you pin the pattern on the cloth carefully as I have written on the pattern, you will find there will be enough cloth for a bonnet, too.
>
> My mother's brother brought this silver thimble to her from England when she was just your age, and she learned to sew with it. I hope you will take good care of it and keep it as long as I have. I learned to sew with it, and your mother used it when she learned to sew, too. It will make me very happy to think you are using it as you

are learning to take small, even
stitches.
Grandmother

"Oh, Mother, isn't Grandmother nice? And only yesterday I thought it was queer she let Abigail start on a long journey without a coat. That's a joke on me!"

"I think it was a very good idea of Grandmother's," answered Mother. "She thought we might be delayed on the road and you would like to have some way to busy yourself."

"My grandmother is the best grandmother in the world! I know she is, and I'm glad I belong to her," said Susan happily, as she began to make the fringe on Abigail's shawl.

The three following days passed quietly. The roads grew worse, so traveling was slow. The men took their turns driving the cows, riding Dan, and driving the oxen.

Susan waved to the children she saw playing out side the few cabins they passed. She often held Abigail up for them to see, and as the wagon jolted, Abigail's head would nod, just as though she, herself, were bowing to the children.

Often they would drive for hours and would see no one. Then Susan amused herself by looking for pictures in the white clouds in the sky. She found that if she looked carefully she could see lovely pictures—sometimes an animal, sometimes a range of high mountains and once she saw clouds that looked exactly like Mary and her little lamb.

CHAPTER VIII
AN OHIO RIVER INDIAN STORY

"Today is the most important day of our trip!" exclaimed Father the morning of the fifth day after they had left their old Kentucky home.

"What happens today?" asked Susan. "Oh, I know; we cross the Ohio River, don't we?"

"That's right. We do. Or rather the ferry takes us across! The 'Hio will be a great sight. You can't imagine such a big river, Susan."

"Is it pretty?" asked Mother.

"No, not exactly pretty," answered Father. "It's too muddy-looking. But that wide expanse of water, almost like a lake, always interests me. Perhaps we will see some of the big river steamboats."

"Let's hurry and eat so we can start," urged James, eager to see the much talked of 'Hio.

With everyone helping, the wagon was quickly packed. "It's amazing to me how fast we can work when there's something ahead we want to see!" exclaimed Father jokingly.

After a few miles, Susan noticed that the wagon had stopped lurching from side to side. The road seemed to be more smooth, and the log cabins were closer together. Across the hills were broad fields and green meadows, while here and there were apple orchards tinged with the soft green of early spring. It was the season of spring rains; the mudholes were full of water, and the brooks were overflowing their banks. The Calvin family rode on in silence, each one waiting for the first glimpse of the great river.

"We're in the 'Hio valley!" finally called James, from where he was riding Dan, far ahead of the covered wagon. "See, they're getting ready to plant tobacco—acres and acres of it."

As the wagon drew up, Susan looked back at the rich flat land. Father drove the wagon a few feet farther to a high, dry portion of the river's bank and came to a stop. He jumped down from the seat, helped Mother and Tim down, and called gaily, "All out! Come and see the big river. Here's a fine view. You'll never forget it." Then he lifted Susan down and led her around the wagon, beyond the team of oxen, where she could see the river.

"There's the Ohio," he said impressively, pointing to the wide, brown river in the distance. "She's not very high now, because we haven't had enough rains, but sometimes I've heard that she rises many feet, overflows her banks, and covers all that fine black earth on either side. The 'Hio is a wicked thing! She whirls and eddies and roars as though she wanted to go higher and higher. Folks have lost their lives fighting her floods."

Susan felt a shiver go up and down her spine as she thought of that powerful river, already as wide as a lake, growing wider and deeper.

The great broad river lay before them. On the farther side there was a range of bluffs which seemed to Susan beautiful banks, rising high on either side.

"What a lot of water!" exclaimed David. "It's almost an ocean."

"Holy Moses!" said James, coming up with the cows. "What a river! Look how it eddies. It must have a powerful strong current."

"You're right, Tom," said Mother softly, "it is

majestic. Isn't this a beautiful valley! But where is Susan?"

"Here I am," came the answer. "I just ran to get Abigail to show her the 'Hio, too."

"That's Madison over there," Father told them, pointing to a group of houses across the river. "We will stop a few hours there for trading. I want to get glass for the windows of our new cabin. We need rope, and we ought to have powder and shot before going on."

"Look! What's that coming down the river?" asked Mother, pointing to a queer boat floating upon the surface of the water with a cabin built in the center.

"Oh, I'm glad we can see that," said Father. "I've heard about them, but I never saw one before. It is called a broadhorn. You know settlers can sometimes travel to their new homes more easily by water than by land. We are traveling by land in a covered wagon. They have built a big flatboat and in the center of it they built a cabin where they live as they travel by water. Look closely, and you can see the cattle back of the cabin. They have a rowboat fastened behind and the washing is hung out to dry."

The Calvins stood watching the queer looking boat as it seemed to drift down the river.

"Look, James," called David, "watch the man standing at the back! See how he guides the boat with that long pole. The whole thing is like a raft, isn't it, Father?"

"Yes, the flatboat is built of big logs. That family will use the deck and sides to make floors for their new cabin. See, Susan, there is a railing all around the edge of the flatboat so that the children and the cattle can't fall into the water."

"Where do you suppose they have come from, Tom?" asked Mother.

"Oh, somewhere back East — maybe as far as Pittsburgh," answered Father. "It used to be very dangerous to travel down the 'Hio River from Pittsburgh, for there was a high rock on the bank not far from Cincinnati where the Indians watched the river night and day. When a boat load of settlers was seen, a band of Indians would often rush down, capture the boat, kill the whites, scalp them, and carry off the boat's cargo. Not so many years ago the Indians were still warlike, and bitterly resented the white man's coming to take more and more of their territory.

"Come and sit down, all of you, on this flat rock, while I tell you a true story," invited Father.

Susan drew close to him, clutching Abigail tightly in her excitement. The eyes of the two boys never left his face. Mother looked off across the river, though her head was inclined to catch every word.

"Some years ago two families were floating down the 'Hio in their flatboats to find new homes. They passed Cincinnati in safety, but one very dark night they were awakened by the cries of Indians, who were holding a war dance around a huge bonfire on the shore. Fortunately, the night was dark and there were no lights on either of the boats.

"They pulled the rear boat loaded with horses, cattle, and live stock, close to the first boat and fastened the two together. Then, hoping that they might not be seen, the little party floated quietly past the scene of the Indian dance. The light of the bonfire was too bright for them to slip by unseen. When the two boats had drifted opposite the fire, the Indians saw them, and ordered them to come to shore and surrender.

"Though the Indians shouted their war cries and used their bows and arrows, the head of the little party whispered to everyone to remain well concealed, and to keep perfectly quiet.

"When the Indians received no answer to their command, they were puzzled. They stopped dancing about the bonfire and shouting. A brief council was held. Then several Indian braves

The little party floated quietly past the scene.

paddled toward them in their canoes. But the two boats floated on, silently, without any sign of life.

"The Indians paddled close. Alarmed by the silence, several halted and allowed their canoes to drift. A few, braver than the rest, circled the two boats. Others came close and peered in. But no one was to be seen, for everybody was carefully hidden. Perhaps the Indians thought it was a boat manned by dead men, for the leader suddenly uttered one word, and then all paddled quickly away, glad to return to their camp fire.

"The little party of white settlers were safe. They cautiously continued their journey and eventually found pleasant homes near one of the settlements in the southern part of Indiana."

"That's the best story I ever heard you tell, Father," said David.

"Did it really happen?" asked Susan.

"Yes, the man who was the head of the party and told everyone to keep perfectly quiet, was the one who told it to me," answered Father.

"I'm glad we're traveling in a covered wagon," said Susan. "I'd rather meet bears than Indians."

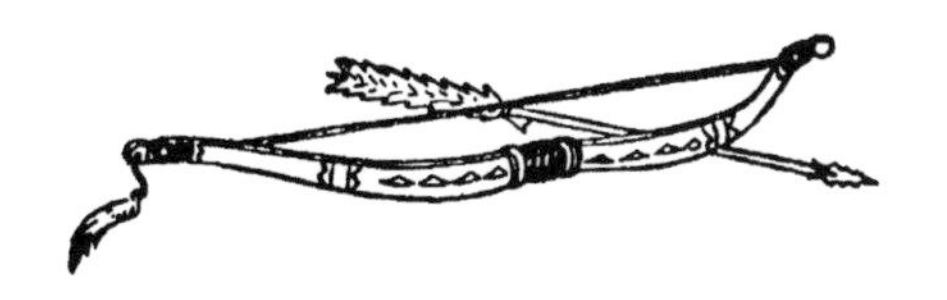

CHAPTER IX
CROSSING THE OHIO RIVER

"Let's drive on down to the river's edge," said Father. "That must be our ferry coming over to this side now."

The family saw a large, flat boat crossing from the opposite shore.

"Bring Abigail and come and sit on the seat between Mother and me, Susan," invited Father. "You must see all that goes on. Dave, put my gun in the back of the wagon. We won't need it in Madison."

"Oh! This is much nicer up here," exclaimed Susan, as she settled herself on the high wagon seat. "I like to see what is coming, instead of what we are leaving behind. Don't you love it, Mother?"

Mother nodded as she watched Father drive the oxen down the steep hill and across the flat river valley to the ferry landing. There was the ferry boat waiting for them.

The ferry was a flat bottom boat that looked to Susan very much like the floor of the biggest store at home. Around this floor was a strong log railing to keep people and animals from falling into the river.

Slowly and carefully Father drove the oxen and wagon on the ferry boat. Dave jumped off Dan's back and led him on the ferry. James drove Buttercup and Molly onto the ferry, while Steve went frisking all over the boat.

"Well," gasped Susan, "I never thought I'd take a wagon ride on a river! Isn't it fun, Abigail?"

From where Susan sat in the wagon she could see a pair of strong ropes attached to one side of the ferry. These were fastened by means of pulleys to a much larger rope which extended clear across the river. Each end of the rope was tied securely to a big pile on each side of the river, but as Father explained, "One pile was in Kentucky, and the other pile was across the river in Indiana."

Two men with strong poles dipped them to the bottom of the river and pushed the flat boat

The ferry was a flat bottom boat.

along. The heavy ropes kept the boat from being pulled from its course by the strong current.

As the ferry drew close to the Indiana shore, James and David slipped between the groups of people, cattle, and packing cases, up to the bow. Here they stood, watching the men on shore tie ropes around the piles on the dock to make the ferry secure. How fast they worked with the ropes, for it seemed that everybody wanted to get off at the same time. Tall negroes were laughing, singing, and pushing each other about as they unloaded bundles of pelts to be shipped to Cincinnati. Bags of wheat and beans, bundles of wool, tall willow baskets—some filled with cheese and eggs—cows, sheep, horses, these all added to the confusion on the dock.

At last it was the Calvins turn to leave the ferry. Father drove the wagon; Dave followed, leading Dan, with Steve close behind him. James shoved and shouted at Molly and Buttercup. The cows slowly looked from side to side, switched their tails, and finally ambled slowly off the ferry.

In the meantime Father had driven across the main street, where he tied the oxen to a hitching post. "Boys," he called, "fasten the cattle to the wagon and give them feed. We will walk around town and do some trading. You boys will want to go down to the wharves to watch the boats load and unload. I suppose Mother and Susan will want to go in the stores. I have business and I want to see an old friend of mine. We will all meet here at the wagon in two hours."

The boys rushed away. Susan picked up Abigail and straightened her bonnet while Mother put on Tim's coat. Then Susan took Mother's hand and walked timidly beside her down the street. It was strange to the child to see so many houses close together, some of which were painted a sparkling white. There were many carriages driving up and down the street, and many people hurrying about. Susan had never seen such a busy place. No one stopped to speak to her, and then she realized that very few people who passed did speak to one another. The men and women were dressed in handsome clothes. Very different from the clothes Susan had ever seen worn.

A flag of red and white stripes with a cluster of white stars on a blue background in one corner was floating over the largest store. Mother and Susan went inside.

The shelves in the front of the store were piled high with the most beautiful cloth. Susan overheard a woman ask to see a "piece of silk," and as she watched the clerk show a lovely shiny fabric with flowers all over it, she kept saying over and over to herself, “Silk, silk.” To Susan it looked like a flower garden in the sunshine.

As Susan and Mother walked slowly toward the back of the store they saw other shelves filled with shoes and boots, and pretty slippers with slim, high heels.

In the back room of the store were things to eat. How good it smelled! There were raisins, kegs of New Orleans molasses, huge cheeses, boxes of salt fish, a crock of pickles, a barrel of coffee, tea, and neat little boxes of spices.

“Mother, what are those pretty yellow balls?” asked Susan, pointing to a basket in which they were piled high.

“Those are oranges, Susan. I haven’t seen any since I left Virginia,” answered Mother.

“What do you do with them?” was the next question.

“Why, you eat them, child. They are very good. I’ll buy one for each of us as a great treat,” and Mother turned to the clerk and bought six.

When Mother paid for them and the clerk handed her the package, they hurried out. They walked past several stores, and at last Mother stopped in front of a window which was filled with bottles — big ones, little ones, and medium-sized ones — each filled with a different colored fluid. Mother explained that it was called an Apothecary Shop, where one could buy every kind of medicine. Susan had never known there were so many medicines in so many colors.

In the next shop window Susan looked longingly at a beautiful pink umbrella with a long white handle.

"That's called a parasol, Susan, and you carry it to keep the sun off your head," explained Mother.

Susan burst out laughing as she asked, "Why should anyone want to keep the sun off? How silly!"

Before Mother could answer, she looked across the street and saw Father talking to a man. He saw them, waved, and both men crossed over to Mother and Susan. He introduced his old friend Frank Gardener to Mother and Susan, explaining, "Frank and I were boys together. Now he lives here in Madison."

"I have been telling Tom," said Mr. Gardener, "that Madison is second only to Cincinnati as a port in the middle west. In one month last year two hundred thousand hogs were butchered and packed here. Madison is often called 'The Gateway to the State' and I like that, don't you?"

From where they stood they could see the big river steamboats lying along the river front, with bags of wheat piled high along the wharves, waiting to be put aboard. "That wheat will be sent as far south as New Orleans, and as far east as Europe," said Mr. Gardener.

A steady procession of covered wagons which looked just like the Calvins' wagon crawled toward the wharves with produce to sell. "They've driven from Indiana down to the Ohio River to ship their goods," he explained, as they watched one wagon unload and saw the men take out bags of wheat, large bundles of straw, and a bag of white beans. "Those two bundles of 'coon skins and that other bundle of muskrat hides will bring a good price," Mr. Gardener added.

"Don't the women send anything to sell?" asked Mother.

"Yes indeed, Mrs. Calvin," replied Frank Gardener. "You'll always find a green willow basket under the driver's seat. In it you'll generally see a roll of blue jeans, some eggs, cheeses, pickles, jelly, and some heavy knit stockings. Oh, yes," he laughed, as he turned to Susan, "there is often a bundle of ginseng roots that the children find in the woods. If you gather any, send it down to me. I'll sell it for you for a good price to someone who will ship it clear to China."

So they talked on about this valley of the 'Hio,

so new to the Calvins, yet so full of opportunity. At last Father asked about the roads into Brown County.

"Most of these wagons turn off before they reach the White River," was the answer. "I understand the roads are passable that far. But from the White River on, there is only a blazed trail into Brown County."

"How about the White River?" asked Father.

"Well, Tom, you really ought to hurry on," was the serious answer. "The White River is high now. The spring rains will soon make it hard to find a place to ford."

Mother sighed, for she knew well the dangers of high water.

Father straightened his shoulders as he said, "In fifteen minutes we meet the boys at the wagon. I've already put in the rope, the powder, the shot, and the glass. We'll leave Madison tonight."

"You'll have good roads for at least two days. I'm sorry to see you hurry through. Look me up when you come back to trade."

"Good by, Frank," said Father, as the two men shook hands.

CHAPTER X
THE STORM

Warm sunshine and fairly good roads made the travel for the next two days unusually pleasant. The oranges which Mother bought in Madison were served as a surprise dessert for Sunday supper, and Sunday evening after prayers, they all sang Mother's favorite hymn again, hoping it would give her the pleasure her surprise gift of oranges had given them.

When Susan woke up Monday morning, she found it cold and dark, with clouds hanging low in the sky. After a hurried breakfast the family pushed on. The roads grew steadily worse as they drove farther and farther from Madison. Soon the road the Calvins were following became little more than a wagon track, as it wound between stumps and boulders, chuck holes and logs.

Woods, woods, woods extended as far as they could see, though perhaps once in the morning and once in the afternoon they would pass a farm, the land partly cleared, with a log cabin in the center of the clearing. The wind moaned through the trees and clutched at the covered wagon, shaking it angrily. Abigail's red sunbonnet blew off. David, plodding along behind with the cows, caught it and handed it to Susan saying, "I found this red bird in a bush! Do you know what to do with it?"

Father watched the clouds settling lower and lower until a gray-green mist seemed to shut them in from the rest of the world. Susan pinned Abigail's shawl about her closely, and tucked her deep in the feather bed. The wagon lurched over a stump in the road, and Susan slid against the old chest.

"Carrie, we are going to have a storm. I believe you and Tim had better get inside the wagon with Susan," she heard Father say above the howling of the wind. He brought the oxen to a stop, helped Mother and Tim down, and walked with them to the back of the wagon.

"Baby Tim and I are coming in here with you, Susan," Mother said anxiously. "Father thinks a hard storm is coming."

"Hop out," called Father in a businesslike way. "I want to make a comfortable place for Mother and Tim in here on the feather bed with you."

Father pushed the furniture back close to the sides of the wagon to make more room. Susan thought of what Mr. Gardener had said a hard rain would do to the White River.

"David, see that the canvas is fastened down tight," directed Father. "James, drive the cattle on as long as you can. If a heavy rain comes and they stop, we'll be stuck here. I'll take care of the wagon."

"Tom, hadn't you better take the chickens out of the coop under the wagon?" called Mother.

Father reached under the wagon and untied the coop. As he took each chicken out, he tied its legs together and tossed it up in the wagon.

Hardly was Father back on the wagon seat when a strong gale caught the wagon, pulling the canvas top so that the ropes screeched with the strain. The wind whistled through the trees, which swayed and bent until it seemed they must snap. The canvas cover shook and pulled until Susan felt sure it would be torn off.

"Mother, I'm afraid the cover will blow off," said Susan.

"You needn't be. Grandfather said it was strong and would stand any wind. Don't you remember how tightly he tied it down, and how carefully he fitted each hoop?" answered Mother.

The wind blew in strange, queer puffs, each stronger than the last. But the canvas top held tight and firm, just as Grandfather had said it would. The sky grew black. Suddenly sharp lightning zigzagged across the sky, illuminating the surrounding forest.

"Abigail, this is the most dreadful storm," murmured Susan. The rest of Susan's sentence was lost in a rumble of thunder that ended with a deep boom. Lightning and more thunder followed. Baby Tim seemed frightened and screamed almost as loudly as the thunder roared, or so it seemed to wide eyed Susan.

Mother leaned over and said between claps of thunder, "The dwarfs are playing at ninepins, Susan." This made Susan smile, for one of her favorite stories was *Rip Van Winkle.*

Then came the rain! At first a few drops struck the canvas top with such force that it seemed as if small stones were being hurled at them by a forest giant. Then came a downpour. The rain swept over them, making the road a river of whirling mud.

"I do believe the rain doesn't stop to come in drops: It just comes in pailfuls," said Susan to Abigail, as she pushed her far under the chest where she couldn't possibly get wet.

The faithful oxen strained on, pulling the wagon through mud that was fast creeping up toward the hubs of the wheels. Looking back, Susan could scarcely see the boys vainly trying to drive Buttercup and Molly in the wagon's wake. They merely stood with their backs to the storm, refusing to move.

"Oh, Mother," shouted Susan above the clap of the thunder and the noise of the rain pelting against the tightly stretched canvas, "look at the mud! David and James are soaked, and the cows won't budge."

Mother's heart sank as she looked back. Mud! Mud! Mud! Could they ever get through it? Mother noticed that the wagon wheels were slipping. Twice the wagon careened against tall trees and the sturdy oxen slipped to their knees

Then came the rain!

again and again. But they struggled up, and trudged slowly on, Father calling to them above the roar of the storm. Foot by foot the wagon lurched forward while Mother and Susan held their breath, feeling that each wagon length forward brought them nearer shelter and safety.

Then came one last lurch — one sudden jerk — and the wagon stood motionless. Mother and Susan looked over Father's shoulder to see the oxen straining to lift their feet out of the mud. The oxen could drag the wagon no farther; even their great strength was powerless against the deep mud.

"Well, we're stopped!" said Father, quietly.

Not a word was spoken as the rain beat on the canvas and the trees screeched and groaned in the high wind. Suddenly they heard a crack — a splintering of wood and a tearing of branches — as a large tree fell in the road directly behind them.

Mother caught her breath. Susan gasped in fright. But in a moment Father appeared at the rear of the wagon. "Well," he shouted, "we're stuck for sure! We can't go forward, and we can't go back. There's nothing to do but wait for the storm to pass. Then we will cut logs and big branches and lay them along this low section of the road. The oxen can walk over a road of branches and pull the wagon, too, without sinking too deep in the mud. There's higher ground ahead. These rains never last long," said Father, as though this were all a part of pioneering.

"Susan, now is a good time for you to cut out Abigail's coat and bonnet and sew on them, isn't it?" suggested Mother.

Susan was glad to have something to do. She found the patterns and the material and cut them out easily, for the wagon was standing still. Soon she began to sew. There was something very comforting about the feel of the little silver thimble on her finger. As Susan made small, even stitches, she wondered to herself how Thurza would have felt if a big forest tree had crashed to the ground just behind her.

After a time the wind gradually died down, and the rain became a gentle spring shower. As Father had said, the storm was passing.

Father, David, and James took out their axes and began to cut down small trees and heavy overhanging branches. After they had cut them, they dragged them into place, and covered the muddy road ahead. Thus, they made a firm footing over which the oxen could draw the wagon without sinking into the apparently bottomless sea of mud beneath. The three men worked steadily, for as Father said, another hard rain would make the road that much worse, and they must get the wagon and cattle to high ground quickly.

"Over beyond that low ridge is the White River; we must make it by nightfall," he said.

In the middle of the afternoon when the rain had stopped, Susan slipped off her shoes and stockings and ran about, helping to carpet the road with the lighter branches which she could carry. The mud felt cold to her bare feet, but it was fun to feel it ooze up between her toes.

Mother smiled as she watched Susan pick her way gingerly among the puddles. Life was hard in this new country, and she believed in letting little girls do lots of things boys did, for they all would have to learn to make the best of hard things.

CHAPTER XI
CROSSING THE WHITE RIVER

Toward sunset Susan went back down the road to bring Molly and Buttercup an armful of sweet fresh grass. "It won't help much with the road," she said to herself after her arms were full, "and how the cows will enjoy it for supper."

She tossed it in a pile in front of them and smiled to see how quickly they swallowed it. As she turned away she saw in the distance a team of oxen wallowing in the mud far down the road over which they had come that morning. She shaded her eyes and looked again.

Sure enough! The oxen were drawing a covered wagon. On it came, but so slowly it scarcely seemed to move. She watched breathlessly as it drew nearer. Suddenly the oxen seemed to sink far down in the mud, and then stand perfectly still. She saw four men climb out of the wagon; in a moment they had their axes, and the sound of chopping filled the air.

"They're stuck, too," exclaimed Susan.

"That is good!" exclaimed Mother when Susan told her of their neighbors. "Many hands will make light work of filling the road, and we can all help each other in crossing the White River, too."

"May I go and see if there are any little girls in the wagon?" asked Susan.

"Yes, run along," answered Mother, "but hold up your skirts so they don't get too wet and muddy."

When Susan came back she told Mother that there were two more wagons which she hadn't seen—three in all—wanting to cross the White River. "They are all old friends, going to new homes together." said Susan. "There are ten children in the three wagons. One of the women, Mrs. Presley, said it would be nice if we could all have dinner together. I said I thought we could eat outdoors on the high ground of the roadside. She told me to ask you if we would join them."

"What a splendid idea!" agreed Mother. "We'll make a jolly time out of what seemed to me this morning might be a real hardship."

Mother pinned up her skirts, took off her shoes and stockings, and climbed quietly out of the wagon, leaving Tim asleep. Susan helped Mother unpack the cooking kettles and food. Then they both went down the road to where a fire was burning and potatoes and venison were roasting. The women and children became well acquainted as they prepared supper, and the men and boys worked together carrying logs and branches to lay across the road.

Mr. Presley had killed a deer the day before, and soon the women were broiling thick steaks of venison over the open fire. Mother brought pitchers of new milk, a crock of yellow butter, and piles of steaming hoecake to add to the feast.

"How far are you folks going?" Father asked, as they were all seated at supper.

"Across the White River and east to Greenfield," one man replied. "Where are you bound for?"

"We're on our way to Jacksonburg, in Brown County. After this rain, I'm wondering if we'll ever be able to ford the White River! What do you think?"

"I dunno! It will be a job all right," was the answer.

The day's heavy work, the good meal, and the warm fire, all made them very sleepy. As soon as the meal was finished each family went back to its wagon to sleep. The stars were twinkling in the clear sky.

"Mother, haven't we had a good time?" asked Susan, as they skirted mud puddles on their return.

The cattle were already asleep, and in a little while all the family was asleep, Abigail in Susan's arms.

By noon the next day the road was ready to use. Father borrowed an extra team of oxen from the Presleys to hitch to the Calvins' wagon. With skillful driving, the family walking, and all the men in the group pushing from the rear, the Calvins' covered wagon was finally pulled to high ground. Then Father unhitched his oxen and loaned them to the other men.

"Calvin, you sure know how to handle those beasts!" said the owner of the next wagon. "I liked the way you got through. I can't do that well! Will you drive my wagon?"

Susan was proud of Father as she watched

him climb on the seat and swing the oxen into line. She was even more proud when the second wagon stood safe beside their own.

"I've heard tell that practice makes perfect," called the owner of the next wagon. "How about trying mine?"

Father drove the next wagon, and the next, down the muddy road, and up the bank. At last the four covered wagons stood in a row, facing the White River. Then the men and boys cheered, but Father laughed, pulled his gray beard and said, "Shucks! Anybody can drive a good team over a good road. We've had the best roadmakers in Indiana working on that stretch of road, and I've never handled finer oxen!"

Not far below them surged the White River, already high on its banks.

"Well, there's nothing to do but ferry the wagons over," said Father to the man nearest. "The oxen, cattle and horses can swim across. I had hoped to ford it, but I'd never risk my wagon in that current! The river's too deep. The first thing to do is to make a raft!"

All the men quickly cut down straight trees of medium size, and hauled the logs to the river's edge. Here they were laid close together, while two men, more experienced than the rest, tied the logs together and bound them securely to strong poles laid across each end of the logs.

"Aren't we going to build any sort of a railing around the raft?" asked David.

"We haven't time," came Father's abrupt answer. "The river has risen a foot since we've been here working. Hitch a pair of our oxen to the raft and drag it into the river. Tie it to yonder tree so it can't get away from you. Put a wagon on the raft and tie it on to stay! One slip is one slip too many, for the wagon will lurch into the river."

Even as Father spoke, the raft was tied to a tree where it rested partly on the bank, and partly in the stream. A covered wagon was rolled onto it, and four men worked at the four corners tying it securely.

"You know, Abigail, that covered wagon waddled down to the raft like a big white duck," said Susan, who sat on a log not far away, holding her doll and watching the preparations.

As Susan watched, Father put the yoke on his oxen. He led them to the river's edge, then out into the stream. Quickly he tied one end of a long rope to the raft, and the other end to the yoke. Then he seated himself between the two oxen on the yoke itself, his arms outstretched with a hand on the neck of each ox.

"Abigail, will you look where Father is sitting to drive those oxen!" exclaimed Susan.

"Are you ready?" shouted Mr. Presley to Father.

"All ready!" came the answer.

"Untie the raft, then," called a second man, "but hold on tight to the rope. Use it to keep the raft from drifting downstream."

As Susan watched, the oxen walked straight into the river. She saw the water creep up above their legs, up their sides, and finally cover their backs. Soon only their heads were above water. Father sat on the yoke, talking to the animals understandingly, she was sure. The raft, with the covered wagon on it, was being pulled straight across the river.

"Just look, Abigail! You'll probably never again see oxen swimming a river and pulling a covered wagon at the same time," said Susan. Abigail looked straight ahead, her blue eyes big and round.

Slowly the oxen swam the river and reached the opposite bank. She watched them wade out, and saw Father jump down from the yoke and untie the wagon from the raft. Then she saw him hitch the oxen to the wagon and pull it up the bank.

At a word from Father the men pulled the

The raft was being pulled straight across the river.

raft back to its starting place, using the rope which they had held all the time. Three more times the trip was made, and soon four wagons stood safe on the opposite bank of the White River.

The women and children who had anxiously watched the ferrying of the first three wagons were all loaded into the last covered wagon to cross.

David drove the horses and cattle into the water, and Susan was surprised to see how well they could swim. But poor Dave, riding Dan, got thoroughly soaked, for only Dan's head and neck were above water, so deep was the river.

That night four covered wagons camped near each other. Susan whispered to Abigail who lay beside her on the feather bed, that while she hadn't really been afraid all day, she was much happier in a covered wagon on land than she was in a covered wagon on water.

Abigail said nothing, so Susan was sure she agreed.

CHAPTER XII
THE ARRIVAL

Early the next morning, after all the good-bys were said, a group of three wagons followed the road northeast to Greenfield. The Calvins' wagon alone followed the mere suggestion of a road straight north to Brown County. The next day the road became only a blazed trail.

For two days more the covered wagon with a chicken coop swinging beneath it followed a blazed trail up thickly wooded hills and down into beautiful, quiet valleys. A bit of bark removed from a tree here and there along the way was the only sign of the road to Brown County in that spring of 1836.

It was late in the afternoon that the Calvins first saw the little village of Jacksonburg nestled snugly in the valley. On the outskirts of the village, and standing quite alone, was a log cabin. The logs were unhewn with the spaces between filled with chips and then chinked with clay.

As the white topped, covered wagon drove up before the doorway, jolly Uncle Sam threw open the door.

"Well, here you are at last! I'm right glad to see you. Ma! Ma! Samanthy! Here they are," he called. "How'd you get through? Roads pretty tough goin'? I hear the White River is as high as it's ever been. How'd you cross it?" he asked, pounding David and James on the back. "Take the cattle out to the shed, boys, and feed them, right out yonder Hop down, Susan! My, how you've grown! You're taller than Samanthy by three inches, I'll be bound," he said, as he lifted her out of the back of the wagon and kissed both red cheeks.

While the men were talking, Aunt Lina took Mother and Tim into the cabin. Susan followed with Abigail and her portmanteau.

"Well, here you are at last!"

"You must be all tuckered out, Carrie!" said Aunt Lina. "Here, give that baby to me and I'll lay him on the bed. He's a husky one, now ain't he! He don't seem a mite tired, do you now, Timmy?"

Tim cooed and gurgled at Aunt Lina as if he had always known her, and Susan felt very proud of her little brother.

"Supper'll be ready right smart now, and you can go to bed early. Get a good rest and then you'll be ready to pick out your new home tomorrow. We'll have to move things about a little to make room for all the beds. If I'd only known when you would get here, I could have had things all ready. But you don't mind, I guess. The men can sleep on the hay in the barn, and with Dave and James sleeping in the loft we'll have plenty of room."

"My goodness, Mother, does Aunt Lina talk that fast all the time? I never heard anybody talk so much," whispered Susan to Mother, as they stood combing their hair and washing for supper.

As Mother made no reply, Susan looked about the cabin. On one side of the room was the great fireplace with its crane, from which hung a steaming kettle. At either side of the fireplace and extending out into the room were wooden seats with high backs to keep off the draughts. From the rafters hung chains of dried apples, and smoked hams and bacon. A square hole was cut in the low ceiling through which the boys would climb when they went to bed in the loft. Through an open door in the end of the cabin, Susan could see the lean-to containing the large loom.

As Susan finished washing, in ran her little cousin Samanthy. She was as plump as her mother. Her smile was just as jolly, and she could talk nearly as fast. She greeted Susan with a hug, and a loud kiss.

"I'm awfully glad you are here, Susan," said Samanthy, putting her arm about her. "We can do everything together, just like sisters, can't we? Come out to the barn with me this minute, and I'll show you my pets. Was it fun coming up? We had a dreadful time when we came. The wagon got stuck in the mud, and we hated it. I got sick, and I'd have given anything to have never started!"

"Oh, I didn't hate it. I liked it most of the time," said Susan. "But you see I had Abigail. Look, Abigail, this is my cousin Samanthy. Samanthy, this is Abigail." Susan held the doll in her arms as she spoke, and Abigail seemed to bow most politely.

"How do you do, Abigail! Oh, Susan, do let

me hold her. I've never had a nice doll in all my life. I only have the things to play with that I make for myself. Where did you get her?" asked Samanthy in one breath, as she took Abigail in her arms.

"Grandmother made her for me, and we've had the most fun together. I'll ask Grandmother if she will make a doll for you, too," Susan added kindly. "She's coming up here to live near us next spring."

Out in the barn Samanthy showed Susan her treasures: the young 'coon her father had caught; the big black crow which was quite tame and would sit on Samanthy's shoulder; the guinea hen which followed her wherever she went; tiny fluffy baby chicks; and, last of all, a big turtle which Samanthy found one afternoon on her way home from school.

Aunt Lina had an excellent dinner for them. "No wonder Sam's so fat!" joked Father, as he took a third piece of dried apple pie, "with cooking like this three times a day."

The next morning everybody was up early and busy with the many chores. Father and Uncle Sam fed the horses and milked the cows, while Dave drove them to pasture and James split the kindling wood. Aunt Lina fried salt pork and eggs in the fireplace for breakfast and Mother stirred up some of her good cornbread which she baked in the reflector, which was a big tin oven.

During breakfast Uncle Sam told them about the land he wanted them to see. "There's good land round about here, Tom, and you could get it easy 'nough, but I've got my eye on the finest piece of land you ever did see. It's up Greasy Creek 'bout two miles. You'll have to clear it, though."

"Oh, we expect to have to clear," answered Father. "I'd rather be away from the village a piece, for we want plenty of room to spread out. I reckon if Dave can find him a wife among these Brown County girls, he'll be getting married one of these days, and the boys and I figure we'd like to get enough land so we can all farm together. We're a homey family, Sam; we like to stay near each other."

"That's just what I said now, isn't it, Lina? Well, I think I know just the piece to answer the purpose. Good rich bottom land, fine for tobacco; fine spring on it, too. There's a pretty hillside, Carrie, where you'll want to build your cabin, and the prettiest hills are around it. Hurry through your breakfast so we can go and look at it."

Uncle Sam pushed back his chair and lighted his pipe while the others hurriedly finished the cornbread and coffee.

Soon Father was ready. "Come, Dave and James, we need you to help pick out the new home site. Carrie, I'll look over several places and then come back for you. Is that all right?" Mother smiled and nodded.

"You and I will ride the horses, Tom," Uncle Sam continued, "and the boys can walk. Be sure to take your guns, boys. You'll find plenty of squirrels up Greasy Creek."

"Lina, let me help you fix things up," said Mother in her sweet way, as the men left. "I don't want to make you any more trouble than I have to! Don't you think if we moved this chair over here and put the table over there, it would give us more room?" she asked, moving the furniture as she talked.

"Sakes alive, Carrie! I've always said you had more sense about fixing up a place than anybody I'd ever seen! Now why didn't I think about changing that chair and table 'round? That's a heap better! Run along, children. Go outdoors to play."

"I'll race you to the barn, Samanthy," called Susan, picking up Abigail and rushing out the cabin door. She was there long before fat Samanthy arrived, and sat watching the old turtle move slowly across the barn floor.

As the two little girls were playing together, Susan suddenly remembered the package her little friend Nancy Kennedy had given her to open the day after she reached her new home. Back to the house she ran to inquire about it. When Mother and Aunt Lina between them found it, Susan hurried back to the barn, anxious to show it to Samanthy.

"Let's go out under the cherry tree to open it," suggested Samanthy. "A barn isn't a nice place to open a present."

Susan untied the red wool yarn that tied it. "Oh, I guessed right," she said delightedly. "The day I got it I guessed it was a basket!"

"I never saw such a pretty basket," exclaimed Samanthy. "It has a handle, too. Do you suppose we could learn to make them, Susan? I would love to have one just like it," and she looked longingly at it.

"Maybe we can! See, Nancy made a pad of pink calico to line the bottom. Her Sunday dress last summer was made of cloth like that pink calico. She's awfully smart! David promised me to make a table for my bedroom next winter when he isn't busy, and then I'll keep the basket on it. Won't that be nice? But in the meantime you may put the basket wherever you'd like, Samanthy.

We'll pretend it's yours!"

'Then we'll both have to write her to thank her, won't we?" asked Samanthy. "We'll do that the very first rainy day."

CHAPTER XIII
NASHVILLE

Before Susan and Samanthy knew it, a big bell sounded, calling them to dinner. When they went in they heard Father telling Mother about the land they had seen that morning up Greasy Creek.

"You'll like it, Carrie, I know. As soon as we finish dinner I want to take you up. I didn't look at anything else, because it didn't seem necessary. No land could be any better than this. It's just what we've wanted. Rich bottom land, plenty of water, good trees! David agrees with me that it's pretty nigh perfect."

Susan had never seen Father so happy. He talked all through dinner telling of the many things he liked about the land.

"I can't see why such good land is for sale!" laughed Mother, as she tried to tease Father.

"May Samanthy and I go to look at the land, Father? Please let us go," urged Susan.

"I reckon so," answered Father. "I can hold you in front of me on Dan. Samanthy can ride with Mother on one of Sam's horses."

Soon after the midday meal, they mounted the horses and rode down the street. Susan looked carefully at the signs over the stores which stood on each of the corners of the crossroads. She spelled out loud: "J-o-e-l S-p-ar-k-e-r G-e-n-e-r-a-l S-t-o-r-e H-a-r-n-e-s-s S-h-o-p P-l-o-u-g-h-s."

"That's the road to Bloomington," Samanthy told them, pointing to the road that led south. "That other road leading over the hill goes to the mill on Salt Creek. Father takes all our corn there to be ground."

Across the road, on the opposite corner, Susan noticed a crowd of people standing outside a store. She wondered what they were waiting for. Then as she read the sign she knew the reason:

EBENEZER WILSON

GROCERIES AND LIQUORS

POST OFFICE

NASHVILLE INDIANA

"There's the post office, Father! Are all those people waiting for letters?"

As she spoke, a man on horseback rode up. Two saddle bags hung across his saddle. He sprang from his horse, lifted off the heavy bags, and carried them into the store. The crowd quickly followed him, all anxious to get their letters and papers.

"I don't understand, Father," said Susan. "I thought Uncle Sam lived in Jacksonburg. That sign reads Nashville. How's that?"

"Oh, I forgot to tell you! When Nashville got the post office, it was decided to change the name of the village from Jacksonburg to Nashville. It hasn't been changed long. Mail is delivered here once a week."

On the third of the four corners Susan spelled out this sign: "J-o-n-a-t-h-a-n W-o-o-l-m-a-n G-u-n-s-m-i-t-h B-l-a-c-k-s-m-i-t-h H-o-r-s-e-s-h-o-e-i-n-g." At one side of the shop she saw a wooden pump and a long trough made from a hollow log.

A man on horseback rode up.

Here the horses were watered.

On the fourth corner stood the meeting house, a long low frame building. Two small windows and two large doors were on the side facing the road.

"What a queer cabin! I never saw one like that. It's like two cabins put together, isn't it? Why did they build it that way?" asked Susan, as they rode past the meeting house and came to this cabin home.

"That's a double log cabin, Susan. It's a good idea. I think I'll build one just like that so next spring I can add on another cabin. That will give us a larger and more comfortable home. Let's stop a minute! I want you and Mother to look at this one carefully."

They saw a double cabin with a passageway between, that was wide enough for a wagon to drive through. Stairs at the back led to the second floor, which extended over both cabins and the passageway.

"There is a fine large cabin of two rooms downstairs, and three rooms upstairs, isn't there, Tom?" asked Mother thoughtfully.

Father nodded as he asked, "Do you know what that passageway is called, Susan?" As Susan shook her head, he continued, "It is called the 'dog trot'." Susan and Samanthy laughed at the funny name.

On they rode, passing several of these double cabins, before they turned to the left and followed Greasy Creek.

"This is Greasy Creek," said Father. "I think we will build near here. Isn't it a fine valley, Carrie?" he asked, as they looked around them.

"I like it very much, Tom. It looks like good land. The view is pretty, too. But there's lots of work to do on this road. It will be bad when it's wet."

"All roads are that way in this new country, Carrie. We'll have to get used to them," agreed Father.

They rode along in silence for nearly a mile when Father turned to the right and climbed to the top of a hill. Here they all dismounted. He tied the horses to the trees, loosened their bridles, and slipped the bits out of their mouths so they could nibble the young grass near them.

"Here is where I want to build," he said. "We can buy all the land we want—mighty good land, too —at a fair price. What do you say, Carrie? How do you like it, Susan? Isn't it a pretty place?"

Susan could tell by Father's voice that he was tremendously pleased. They stood looking over the flat rich land with the beautiful hills all about them without speaking. The quiet beauty of the place impressed them all.

"Tom, see how blue the hills look," said Mother, "a misty blue. It will be peaceful living here. I'm very glad we came."

Then she and Samanthy and Susan sat down on a fallen log to enjoy the view.

"How much is it an acre?" asked Mother practically.

"Sam tells me about two dollars. We have nearly three hundred dollars left. We were in luck to get that good price for our farm in Kentucky. I've a mind to buy a fairly large piece of land, one that would cost about a hundred-and-sixty-dollars. I could pay cash for that. Then we could buy more when our first crops are sold, and we have the money. I don't want to spend all our money for land though, for we want to buy pigs, and there'll be food to buy until our crops are harvested. What do you think, Mother?"

"Tom, we must buy sheep, too; we'll need wool for our clothes. Didn't you say you needed another horse?"

So they sat on the log and talked in the warm spring sunshine. The birds sang, the flowers bloomed, and Father and Mother were very happy planning.

At last it was decided to take a whole section of land and to build on the hill, because as Father pointed out, the valley might be flooded each spring when Greasy Creek overflowed its banks. The low land would be that much the richer and would grow fine tobacco or make good pasture land. As soon as the hillside could be cleared, Mother wanted to have apple trees planted.

"There's something so lovely about an apple orchard in bloom, Tom," she said. "I feel sure apples would do well on these hills."

CHAPTER XIV
ON A HILLTOP

When they returned they found that David and James, with Uncle Sam's help, had sharpened the axes. Early the next morning the men left to begin cutting logs for the new cabin on the hilltop.

Mother, Aunt Lina, Susan, and Samanthy stayed home to wash, for as Susan said, "Even Abigail's clothes need to be washed! Traveling does get one so dirty."

"You have to excuse me," she said to Abigail, "if I don't dress you this morning. I'm going to wash your clothes and you'll have to stay in bed until they are dry and ironed. When the first rainy day comes, I'll make you a new dress to wear when the one you have on is in the wash."

It was long after dinner before Susan found time to dress Abigail, for baby Tim was cross that morning, and Susan had all she could do to care for him and hang up the clothes.

Uncle Sam had driven two large forked sticks in the ground and put a strong green pole across them. Here on the pole was hung the big black kettle, where the water for washing the clothes was heated. Samanthy brought the water from the well, and made three trips to the woodpile for chips and logs for the fire.

"Here, Samanthy, take this crock of soft soap I just made and put it on that stump," called her mother. "Carrie'll need a right smart lot of soap for that mess of clothes. Give me a hand with these tubs, will you? Dearie me, how heavy these wooden tubs are. Say, Carrie, remember to throw all the dirty water on the flower beds as long as you're here, won't you? Water gets awful scarce round here in the summer." Aunt Lina seemed to talk continually.

By early afternoon the clothes were waving on the clothes line, looking almost as though there were people inside them, Susan thought to herself. She was combing Abigail's hair and putting on her clean dress and pantalets. Only her shawl, coat and bonnet were in her portmanteau, and Susan had left that open in the sun all morning to give it a good airing.

When Mother called Susan the next morning she snuggled down further in bed, closed her eyes, and said, "I don't feel well at all! I don't know what's wrong."

Mother came over and looked down at her carefully. "Land sakes, child, you've got the yellow jaundice," she exclaimed. "You're all yellow. Even your eye balls are yellow." Then she walked toward the fire and called, "Oh, Lina! Susan's got the jaundice. Have you any of those bitters Grandmother used to give us?"

"Course I have, I couldn't keep house without those bitters!" answered Aunt Lina. "Samanthy, climb up and get the bottle. It's on the top shelf of the cupboard."

"There's only a tiny bit left," called Samanthy, handing the bottle down to her mother.

"I recollect now, Sam had a tough case o' jaunders 'bout a year ago and used most of it up. I meant to make more, but I clean forgot it. Here, Susan, you take this spoonful and I'll make more right away."

Aunt Lina held up the bottle and Susan watched her pour out some dark green medicine.

"I'd rather have the jaunders than take any of that awful stuff!" exclaimed Susan, beginning to cry.

"I think you must be tired out from your journey, if you cry so easily," Mother said quietly. "You will have to stay in bed for a few days, take the medicine, and get a good rest. Then you will get well, and be a happy little girl again. Father will want you to go to the clearing with him. Now brace up."

Susan swallowed the medicine, and found to her surprise that it didn't taste as bad as she had imagined.

"Where do you suppose I put that recipe for the jaunders medicine?" Aunt Lina asked herself, as she stood with her hands on her hips, trying to remember. Going over to the big family Bible which lay on the mantle, she turned through the pages until she found the piece of paper for which she was looking.

Then she read aloud:

> Remedy for Yellow Jaunders
>
> Take a double handful of dewberry roots, a double handful of roots of cranebill, two

> gallons of witch hazel leaves. Boil these separately until the juice is entirely extracted. Strain, and pour out all the liquid into one vessel. Boil this down to a quart. Add a pint of good French brandy and a pound of sugar. Dose: One teaspoonful every hour.

Aunt Lina paused; then she said, "I haven't half the stuff to make it with, but I know what we'll do! Samanthy, you run up to old Mrs. Scroggins. She's a good herb doctor, half Indian, and tell her your cousin Susan from Kentucky took sick with the jaunders, and we are all out of medicine. Ask her if she will lend us some, please. Now, mind you're polite! Take her along that apple pie I baked last night. It's a right smart piece up Clay Lick. You be spry now, Samanthy, and don't spill the bitters."

Samanthy was successful in bringing home the bitters, and for days Susan took the medicine regularly while her skin cleared and she grew to be once more the wholesome, happy child who had left her home in Kentucky.

At last she was well enough to go with Father, David, and James, to spend the day at the clearing on the top of the hill. Samanthy brought out a basket and they packed their lunch, so they could stay all day. With Samanthy carrying Abigail, and

Susan carrying the lunch basket, they started.

On the way Father told them about a strange old man — he called him a "queer old codger" — who lived halfway up Greasy Creek, all alone in a rough, half-faced cabin. "He's lived around here for years and years, he isn't related to anybody, and he spends most of his time trapping and hunting over the hills. I imagine he knows lots of good stories, though," Father ended.

Sure enough, deep in the valley the girls heard someone chopping wood. Father turned off the road, and the three followed a little path through the woods.

CHAPTER XV

A GOOD NEIGHBOR

"Hello, neighbor," called Father when he came within sight of the cabin. The chopping ceased and the queerest old man with a long white beard came to meet them.

"Hi," he said. "Got the young 'uns with ye, have ye? That's good. I always like young 'uns! Howdy, gals."

As he shook hands with Susan he said, "You was the one that was sick, wasn't you? I ken tell by lookin' at ye. Jaunders makes a person mighty sick, but not so bad as fever'n'agur. I had a powerful bad spell of that last spring. Couldn't stop a shakin'. You go on to your chopping and I'll send the gals up after a spell," he said to Father, as he turned toward his cabin with a little girl on either side.

"My name is Jake Schoonover, but all the young 'uns call me Uncle Jake," said he. "I like little gals, and posies. We'll see each other often."

Soon an opening in the woods appeared at the end of the path. Here was a garden spot, and a crude kind of shed, the half-faced cabin Father had spoken about. Logs formed three sides of the cabin; the fourth side had no wall, but was covered with a curtain made of animal skins sewn together. The ceiling was low and made of rough clapboards laid upon poles which served for joists. From these joists, as Uncle Jake called them, many things were hung: hunks of jerked beef, links of homemade sausage, bunches of dried catnip and fragrant camomile and pennyroyal, strings of red peppers used to make certain medicines, and ears of choice seed corn.

He had made a bed over in the corner by laying a pile of branches along the wall and covering them with moss and leaves. Over this was thrown a blanket. Against the opposite wall were a table and chair. There was no fireplace, for he told the girls he did all of his cooking over an open fire in front of the opening of the shack.

"Here, Snooper, come and speak to the ladies," he called, as a large brown hunting dog came around the corner of the shack.

"What beautiful brown eyes he has," said Susan, as she patted the dog's head. "He's the kindest looking dog I ever saw."

"Snooper looks kind all right, but he's a ferocious fighter, Snooper is," said Uncle Jake. Then he told them how every day in the winter he and Snooper went to each of his traps to see what might be in them. "I salt the skins and dry 'em, and send 'em to Madison to sell; but trappin's about over this year. Gettin' too warm! Ye know in warm weather the animals shed their fur and I can't sell the skins for much, so in summer I work in my garden patch, grow my pretty posies, and 'taters, and things.

"Your pa'll be wonderin' where ye be, gals. Maybe we'd better be goin' up toward his place now. Bring your ma down some day and I'll give her some 'yarb' roots for her garden. I got a lot o' healin' 'yarbs' fer sickness. Does she like sassafras tea? I'll bring 'er up some sassafras, if she does. Now go along up the road. Ye can hear your pa choppin' up yonder. Come and see me whenever ye can, gals."

"Thank you, Uncle Jake, we've had a very pleasant time. We'll be glad to come again and bring Mother," said Susan.

The girls found Father and then wandered about in the woods, looking at the lovely spring flowers and listening to the calls of the birds.

"Abigail, you sit down under this tree while we cross the brook," said Susan, who by this time was carrying her. "Then Samanthy and I can carry the lunch basket between us."

She left Abigail comfortably seated with her back against an old sycamore tree, with a wild rose bush to keep the sun off. From there Susan and Samanthy went farther and farther down the hill to the spring at the very bottom. After they had made cups of their hands and had a drink of the cold water, they sat down on the grass to eat their lunch.

Through the long sunny afternoon they picked spring flowers for a big bouquet for Mother and Aunt Lina. Susan taught Samanthy how to weave a basket of grasses, and by the time it was finished and the spring flowers were arranged in it prettily, it was sunset, and Father was calling them to go home.

She left Abigail seated against an old sycamore tree.

Mother and Aunt Lina were delighted with the basket of flowers. Aunt Lina put it in the middle of the table for dinner and spoke again and again of how pretty it was, how smart the girls were to make the basket, and how glad she was to have Susan here for Samanthy to play with.

The day in the clearing had made Susan very tired and sleepy, so she went to bed the moment she finished dinner. By the time Mother and Aunt Lina had washed the dishes and Mother went over to Susan's trundle bed to see that she was well covered, Susan was sound asleep.

"Poor child! She must have been tired," sympathized Aunt Lina. "Here she is, just over the jaunders, and I'll wager she and Samanthy walked five miles today, hunting flowers for us! Well, a good night's sleep will be the best thing for her," of a sound sleep. She heard Steve barking, and she wondered sleepily whether he had treed a 'coon. Then she reached out in the dark to be sure that Abigail was comfortable.

"Abigail, where are you?" whispered Susan, feeling under the quilt for her. She could not find her. Susan sat up in bed. On the floor beside her was Abigail's portmanteau, but no Abigail!

In a flash Susan remembered—she had left Abigail sitting all alone under a tree in the woods.

"Oh, dear! Oh, dear! What will Abigail do!" she thought. "Perhaps a bear will come and carry her away. Now it is raining. Abigail will get wet. How could I have forgotten her!"

Susan began to cry—great big sobs—and the more she cried, the worse she felt. At last Mother heard her sobbing, and came over to find out what had happened.

"Susan, whatever is the matter? What has happened? Stop crying and tell Mother, dear," she said, taking Susan in her arms. Mother sat down in the old rocker with the little girl on her lap and talked soothingly until Susan could tell her how she had left Abigail under a tree in the woods all alone.

"I don't know which tree, or where it was in the big woods," Susan ended with a sob.

"Well, that was careless," agreed Mother, "but you can go with Father the first thing in the morning and get her. I'm sure you can find her with Samanthy's help. There will probably be a little path through the grass where you two children walked. I'm quite sure you can find Abigail. We'll all help, if necessary."

"But you don't understand, Mother. You see I haven't any idea what tree I left her under! How can we find her? Abigail must be cold and wet, and dreadfully frightened all alone in the big woods," sobbed Susan.

"You get back in bed now," said Mother firmly. "I'll sit down beside you for a little while and you must stop crying and go to sleep!"

It was nearly an hour later when Susan's sobs grew less, and the tired little girl went back to sleep.

CHAPTER XVI
WHERE WAS ABIGAIL?

In the morning she asked Mother not to tell anyone about it until she had tried to find Abigail. "I'm so ashamed of my carelessness," she whispered.

Mother and Susan went out to the barn to find Father, but Uncle Sam told them the men had left earlier than usual that morning, and had been gone quite a while.

"Sam, may I take your horse for a bit? I want to ride up to the clearing to see Tom," Mother said quietly.

"Sure you can! Dolly's as gentle as a lamb. You can ride her easy," said Uncle Sam, putting on the saddle and bridle.

"Come, Susan, I want you to go with me. Run and tell Aunt Lina we are going, and ask her to please listen for Tim."

"My! Isn't Mother good!" thought Susan, as she ran into the cabin.

There was almost a smile on Susan's face as she perched herself up in front of Mother on Dolly's back.

"Now, Susan, can't you remember which way you went? Try hard to think," said Mother when they reached the clearing and she was tying Dolly to a tree.

Susan thought it was down toward the big walnut tree, but she wasn't very sure. So Susan and Mother walked up and down, back and forth for more than an hour, looking for Abigail. Even Mother began to get discouraged.

"Susan, I must go back to feed Tim," she said at last. "I don't know just how we are going to find Abigail. We can't ask Father and the boys to stop their work to help us hunt. Aunt Lina is too fat to climb over these hills. I can't ask her to care for Tim again this afternoon. Hadn't we better tell the family about it, and then as the men are working they can be looking for her. You and Samanthy can come back this afternoon and go on looking. We will find her." Mother spoke with such certainty in her voice that Susan felt much better.

There was no one who could stop work to take Susan and Samanthy back to the clearing after lunch, so they decided to walk. When they arrived at the clearing they were so tired that Samanthy said she couldn't walk another step "even if Abigail belonged to her."

Susan set off by herself. She looked under each tree, and all around the trees. There was no Abigail. She looked under all the bushes and in the tall grass. There was no Abigail. But on and on she went in her search. All the long afternoon she hunted until she heard Father whistle. The day's work was ended, it was time to go home; slowly and sadly she went back to Father.

All the next day Susan and Samanthy hunted for Abigail, without finding her. That night Susan couldn't eat any supper. Every bite she took stuck in her throat.

"I'll tell you what I'll do," said Father finally, "I'll write Grandmother. The mail leaves day after tomorrow. I'll ask her to make you another doll. How's that, Susan?" and Father leaned back smiling, thinking he had fixed the trouble.

"Oh, no Father! That wouldn't help. Another doll! That isn't Abigail," said Susan, as she burst out crying and ran away from the table and outdoors.

Father looked at Mother as he said, "I'm afraid the child is making herself sick." Mother looked at Father very seriously and replied, "I know just how she feels. Rachel gave Abigail such a real face. Susan has never had a sister, and Abigail has come to be a very real person to her. I'm afraid there is nothing we can do except help her forget Abigail, and after a time I hope she won't feel so terribly."

"I've offered her my 'coon, or my turtle, or even my guinea-hen," said Samanthy sadly, "but she won't take them. All she does is think about Abigail. I feel so sorry, for I think almost as much of Abigail as Susan does."

The next evening, just as the family was sitting down to supper, there came a rap at the door.

"I wonder who's coming at this time o' day," said Uncle Sam, going to the door and opening it. "Well! Well! If it isn't Uncle Jake. Howdy, neighbor. Come right in."

"Oh, Abigail!" shrieked Susan, who had been standing near the door and was very close to Uncle

Jake when he stepped in. "Oh, Abigail," she said again softly, as she clutched her doll from under Uncle Jake's arm and stood hugging it tightly. "Where did you find her, Uncle Jake? Where did you find her? I looked everywhere in the woods."

"Come in, Uncle Jake! Come in, and draw up a chair and have a bite with us," urged Aunt Lina.

"Thank ye, thank ye kindly, but I'll be goin' back. I thought the little gal would want her doll."

"Oh, come now, draw up to the table with us and have some o' Lina's biscuits. You never ate better!" urged Uncle Sam. "Where'd you find Abigail? We've been 'bout crazy over here since she was lost!"

Noticing Uncle Jake's puzzled expression, Mother hastened to explain that Abigail was the name of Susan's doll which he had just brought in.

Then Uncle Jake in his queer way told them how his good dog, Snooper, had come in with the doll in his mouth at sunset three days ago. "I calls him Snooper 'cause he's allus snoopin' 'round and findin' things," he said by way of explanation. "I've been mighty busy gettin' my 'coon skins ready to sell, so I couldn't bring the doll back until tonight. I set her up on a shelf, and she was lots of

"Where did you find her, Uncle Jake?"

company. She looked that natural, it'll be kinda lonesome without that nice little gal with me. I wanted to keep her, but I 'lowed little Susan would be lonesome fer her, so I brung her down."

Uncle Jake did stay long enough to have as many of Aunt Lina's biscuits as he could eat. As he left, Susan went over to him, her face beaming with happiness, and Abigail held tightly in her arms. "Thank you, Uncle Jake! Thank you a hundred times for bringing Abigail back to me," she said.

After supper as Susan sat in the firelight close to Mother with Abigail in her arms, she was very quiet.

"Why so still, Susan?" asked David, pinching her cheek. "I am surprised that you aren't hopping up and down with joy."

"I am happy, Dave," she anwered, "but I was just thinking how foolish it was for me to worry and carry on so about Abigail. It really didn't help a speck. So I made up a poem about it.

IT DOESN'T PAY TO WORRY

It doesn't pay to worry,

'Cause it only makes it worse!

But when you're thinking happy thoughts

It's like money in your purse.

I've known that if you worry

You'll never find the clue.

So now let's all stop worrying

And the Lord will see us through.

—Emily Sperry

CHAPTER XVII
BORROWING FIRE

With the finding of Abigail, quiet and happiness once more settled over Uncle Sam's cabin, and the days passed quickly for Susan. She helped to care for baby Tim, while Mother cooked and kept the cabin in order. It was Mother's suggestion that she do the work inside so that Aunt Lina could work outdoors in her garden—her kitchen garden as she called it—for Aunt Lina was noted in the little village of Nashville for her early vegetables and flowers. The first sweet peas always came from Aunt Lina's garden.

"Folks do say I raise the most beautiful sweet peas hereabouts," she confessed to Mother. "It makes no difference what the weather is, I plant sweet peas on the seventeenth of March, rain or snow. Last year on the seventeenth, I shoveled away the snow to dig the trench for the sweet pea seeds. I was a bit worried about putting them in, but it worked out all right. The blooms were the finest I've ever raised!"

One Wednesday Mother and Susan were left alone with Tim, for Uncle Sam, Aunt Lina, and Samanthy went to get sweet potato plants.

As soon as they had waved good-by Mother said, "Susan, if you will wash the dishes I'll finish threading the loom. Lina says I may have all the balls of carpet rags she has sewn to use in a rug for our new cabin. We will have to work fast to get it finished by the time of the housewarming, but we can do it if you will help. It is very easy to learn how to weave after the loom is threaded. I'll finish the threading, start the weaving, and then you can work at the loom while I do the baking."

"Oh, goody! I've always wanted to weave! I'll get the dishes washed before you can say Jack Robinson," cried Susan happily.

Susan could soon hear a *bang, bang, bang* resounding through the cabin. Then she knew that

Mother had finished threading the loom and had begun to weave.

"Why, Mother, what a lot you have done already!" exclaimed Susan, as she stood in the doorway of the lean to a half hour later, watching her mother. "You've woven 'most a foot."

"Oh, weaving rugs is quick and easy!" encouraged Mother. "Your arms may get tired beating, but it's very important to beat well, for that makes a firm rug. We don't want any loose weaving. These rags aren't as heavy as I wish they were. Good firm material in the rags does so much to make a good rug. But I'm mighty thankful to have these rags sewn, ready for use. It was good of Lina to give them to me. I'll return the same number of balls of rags to her as soon as I get them. She doesn't need them now, and we do!"

"This loom isn't like ours, is it, Mother?" It's bigger and heavier! This one is so clumsy looking! Can't we set up ours?"

"Oh, no! Father hasn't time to set up ours now. Don't you remember how long it took him to get it apart to put into the wagon. Come over here, and I'll let you begin to weave."

Susan sat Abigail down near the loom and climbed up on the stool where her mother had been sitting. But when she tried to reach the treadles of the loom she found her legs were too short.

"I can't reach; how can I weave?" asked Susan sadly.

"Oh, dear! I never thought of that. You'll just have to stand up, Susan. It'll be harder, but you can manage. When David has time, he will make you your own weaving stool that will be just the right height. I want to teach you to weave linsey-woolsey, too. You and I will need new dresses and you can help me to weave the cloth. We'll wait to do that until after we shear the sheep next spring, and then we can use our own wool."

As Mother talked, she sorted out the balls of rags piled high in a basket near the loom. "I want you to use dark rags, with some bright red. This rug we're working on will be laid in front of the door, and it will have hard wear. We have the bear skin for the floor in front of the fireplace.

"In weaving, the important thing to remember is the edge. You must keep a straight edge. If you pull too tight, the edge will draw in; and if you don't pull tightly enough, the edge of the rug will stretch and then the shape of the rug will be crooked and look badly. Watch carefully, Susan! Push the left treadle down with your left foot; throw the shuttle through with your left hand; catch it with your right hand, like this." Mother easily and quickly showed Susan as she talked.

"Then step on the right treadle with your right foot; throw the shuttle through with your right hand; catch it with your left! It's very easy! Now you try."

But when Susan tried, the shuttle instead of flying through as Mother's had done, stopped halfway. Susan looked up at Mother in dismay.

"Never mind, push it the rest of the way with your hand, Susan. It takes practice of course. Keep at it, and you will get so you can throw it all the way through. Now I'm going to set the bread! I want to get it baked before noon. Call me if you need me." Away hurried Mother, leaving Susan alone with Abigail and the loom.

"Abigail, I don't know whether this is going to be as much fun as I thought. It seems like hard work to me!" said Susan, as she looked into Abigail's blue eyes.

Try as hard as Susan would, the shuttle would not fly all the way through, and Susan's arms ached from pulling the heavy wooden bar back after each strip of cloth had been woven through. "I can't give up, though," she thought. "We need this rug and Mother will never have the time to do it all herself." Then she worked harder than ever at the big loom.

She worked harder than ever at the big loom.

"Susan! Susan!" called Mother, with something in her voice which made Susan drop the shuttle and run to where she was standing before the fireplace. Mother's hands were raised in horror, and a look of amazement was on her face.

"The fire is out! There's not one single live coal left, not even a spark. How could I have forgotten it! I've never let the fire go out before, and it's nearly time for me to start dinner. How could I have been so careless?"

"It's because Aunt Lina always takes care of the fire, and you have gotten out of the habit, Mother," said Susan practically. "Never mind, I'll go and borrow some coals from Uncle Jake. It won't take long for me to run over to his cabin. It's halfway to the clearing. We'll have dinner in time, you just see! I'll run very fast."

"You are a comfort, Susan. Of course we can borrow some live coals. Take the small iron kettle; put some ashes in it, and hurry along. Uncle Jake will know how to fix the coals so that they will burn until you get back. Do be careful. Don't fall, carrying those hot coals. Don't tarry, Susan, we must have dinner ready when the men get home, for Father begrudges every minute he isn't working on the cabin."

Susan shoveled ashes from the fireplace, put them in the smallest iron kettle, and ran quickly down the road.

"No fire in the fireplace!" thought Susan. "How strange!" Never in her life had she known a fireplace to be cold. Summer or winter, a small fire was always burning day and night, so that the meals could be cooked. Father and Grandfather were skillful in raking the ashes over the fire at night so that it would give very little heat. Yet in the morning all that was needed was to have the ashes raked away from the coals, a little kindling wood laid on them, and the coals would burst into a fine blaze.

"I wish I didn't have to tell Uncle Jake that Mother let the fire go out. He might think Mother careless. He hasn't known Mother very long, not long enough to know how smart she is, and how she never forgets things. I guess I'll let him think I let it go out," Susan thought jerkily, as she ran on her errand.

When Susan reached Uncle Jake's cabin she found him cooking potatoes over a fire in the yard. He was smoking his corncob pipe and Snooper lay nearby.

"Our fire has gone out. May I borrow some coals from your fire please, Uncle Jake?" Susan drew a long breath. She hadn't said Mother had let the fire go out, and neither did she have to tell a lie. How lucky!

"Borrow coals from my fire? Well, well, well! Now that is a bad fix to be in. I remember when I was a little shaver our fire went out one night when it was so cold that the water froze in the trough in the barn. But pappy had his tinder box and flint and steel, and the next mornin' he soon had a spark, and a new fire a-goin'." Uncle Jake laughed at the recollection.

"Brought a kettle along, did ye? That's good. Come over here and we'll see what we can do."

He filled Susan's small iron kettle halfway full of ashes. Then he carefully placed a shovel full of red hot coals on top of the ashes. He covered the glowing coals with more ashes and packed them down hard. Then he put the lid on the kettle and handed it to Susan, saying, "Take hold of the handle and walk careful! Don't fall and don't spill the coals. By the way, how's Abigail? Bring her along the next time ye come."

"Thank you, I will; and we surely do thank you for the fire," Susan remembered to say.

"Tell your paw to come and set a spell and visit some day, will ye? Have you got your cabin most done?"

"Yes, sir, we think we'll move in next Monday. Father says we're going to have a housewarming after we get in. We hope you'll come. It's going to be an all day party and the men will help put up the barn. I must hurry. Good-by. Thank you." And away went the little girl skipping down the path.

"Susan, Susan," called Uncle Jake. "Have a care. Ye'll spill the coals sure."

But Susan was out of hearing.

"Nice little gal. Nice family, those Calvins. I'm glad they came to Brown County. They're good folks to have here," thought Uncle Jake as he began to refill his pipe and look at the 'taters.

It took Mother only a few minutes to start the fire with the coals Susan brought, and soon dinner was cooking in the fireplace.

Mother told them all at dinner about her carelessness. Father laughed and said, "I wish I had bought some of those new things I saw in Madison. We ought to have them in the house for just such an emergency. You remember, Carrie. They are very small pine sticks with sulphur on one end. Lucifer matches they're called. You strike one on the sulphur end against something rough and it bursts into a flame. Keep them in the house, and you're never without fire. How's that for a wonderful invention, boys?"

"It doesn't sound true to me," said James. "I wish I'd seen them. I'll have to see someone make fire that way before I'll believe it."

"All right! I'll tell you what I'll do," answered Father, "if we have a good crop this summer, I'll buy a bunch of Lucifer matches—there's a hundred in a bunch—when we go to Madison next fall to trade, and you may light the first one, James."

CHAPTER XVIII
A HOUSEWARMING

The days passed quickly. From sunrise to sunset the boys and Father cut logs of uniform size for the cabin. Four of the straightest, strongest logs were laid as the foundation with heavy puncheons across them for the floor. With Uncle Sam's help, the log walls were raised higher and higher, and the space between the logs securely chinked with chips and clay. In building the cabin they were careful to leave spaces for the doors and windows. Large stones in the woods or pastures were collected and used to build the generous fireplace.

A plot of ground close to the cabin was cleared — even the roots of the trees and the old stumps had been pulled out — and the ground made smooth and level for a garden. A fence of stakes driven close together that was higher than Susan was tall, had been built around the garden plot.

Susan, who had been watching David drive in the stakes, asked, "Why do you stop to build a fence when there's so much else to do?"

"Look around you, Susan," answered David kindly. "See the hawks circling above. Look at that black cloud of birds over yonder. They're crows. There's a rabbit sitting on that log watching us. I've seen a 'coon run up that tall tree several different times. Watch carefully and you'll see a fox and deer in that strip of woods yonder. There are squirrels everywhere. The men in the village tell me they often hear the call of wolves on a winter night. We must protect our garden from all these wild creatures.

"And, Susan, have you noticed how Father is constantly burning up all the piles of brush and rubbish? That's because snakes hide in them. I don't want to frighten you, but there are plenty of snakes here abouts, so you'd better watch out!"

On that same day Susan and Samanthy were eating their lunch, when Susan said happily, "We're going to have a double cabin when Father has time to build it. Then Abigail and I will have our own room. Mother said I might have pink curtains, and I'm going to ask Grandmother to put a pink border around the patchwork quilt she's making for me. Some day I'll weave a pink rag rug, too. Won't that be fun?"

"Yes," agreed Samanthy, "and you have a pink quilted pad in the bottom of the basket Nancy Kennedy gave you. Your room will be so pretty!"

Early on a Monday morning Father hitched up the oxen and piled the covered wagon high with every piece of furniture they had brought from Kentucky. All was ready to drive to the new home. The Saturday before, he and mother had bought a heavy black walnut bed for Susan, a table, and several other pieces of furniture from a neighbor who was moving away. These pieces were already in place in the cabin home.

Susan with Abigail and her portmanteau started on ahead of the wagon for, as she explained, "I can't wait to get there to look around and get ready for company. Today's the day of the housewarming, Abigail. I'm glad your clothes are clean."

As the little girl and her doll approached the new cabin that was to be their home, the sun shone on the two glass windows on either side of the front door so brightly that they seemed to glow in welcome.

Susan and Abigail wandered about the cabin and were there to watch Father unload the wagon. First came the cherry bedstead and the feather bed, on which they had traveled so comfortably. Then Mother's rocker was taken out and placed in the cabin near the fireplace. Her treasured candlestand was put close to it, and Mother, herself, put the brass candlestick on the mantle.

She smiled as Father laid the bear skin rug in front of the fireplace while he sang,

Heigh o! the derry oh,
Mother killed a bear.

The bureau from Kentucky was set against the far wall. David put the Seth Thomas clock on the mantle carefully, wound it, and at once it began ticking out the cheery song Susan had always heard in Kentucky.

Father hung the big, black pot on the crane in the fireplace. He kindled a fire, using the chips Susan and Samanthy had gathered while the logs for the cabin were being squared. Hardly was a fire blazing in the new fireplace, when the first neighbor arrived for the housewarming, as Mother called it, or the barn raising as Father called it. That neighbor was Uncle Jake. He appeared at the door with a fine deer thrown over his shoulders.

"I reckon ye could use this for venison stew," said he, and James and David grinned with pleasure as they quickly took it from him, and began dressing it.

"Where's Susan?" he asked.

"Good morning, Uncle Jake, I'm glad you've come," said Susan running up. "I got home with the fire all right."

"Good morning," said Mother, before he could reply. "We brought coals from that same fire with us, and we've just used them to start the fire in our new home. So thank you again."

"I'll always be glad to know that, ma'am," said Uncle Jake. "Ye're right fine neighbors. I'm glad ye're here! But, Susan, here's somethin' for Abigail. She's been purty busy and it 'pears to me she needs a comfortable place to rest!" Uncle Jake handed Susan a doll bed, made of hickory wood and perfectly finished. "I began makin' it for her when Snooper first brought her to my cabin. All I could do then was set her on a chair, but now she can lie down when you think she's tired!"

"Uncle Jake, you're really the nicest person," said Susan. "Thank you very, very much. I'll piece a quilt for her bed just as soon as I can."

Susan laid Abigail down, and Uncle Jake smiled with satisfaction as he saw how very comfortable Abigail seemed to find her new hickory bed.

"Now I've brought my ax," said he, turning to Father. "I've come to help build yer barn. Suppose we go out and get busy."

Uncle Sam, Aunt Lina, and Samanthy drove up as Uncle Jake walked toward the pile of logs that were soon to become the barn.

"I've brought a crock of pickles, jars of preserves, and two cakes, Carrie," called Aunt Lina. "Here's my quilting frame. Sam, don't you be agoin' toward that barn before you help me get it in place."

Uncle Sam laughed pleasantly as he helped Lina set up the frame in the shade of a tall tree.

"Here, Carrie, is a quilt I've pieced," said Aunt Lina, as Mother came out to meet them. "I have all the materials, too, and we women folks will quilt it today. See! It's my favorite pattern."

Susan looked at Aunt Lina and Samanthy in amazement. Tears of pleasure gathered in Mother's

Susan laid Abigail down.

eyes as she said, "But, Lina, all that work! You shouldn't!"

"Why not?" asked Aunt Lina happily. "I worked on it all winter long, hoping I could use it for this very thing — a housewarming for you. You don't know how I wanted you folks to come! See, it's the wild goose pattern. Many's the time I've looked out of my cabin to see a flock of wild geese flying overhead that looked just like this."

"Of course," said Mother, "each patch of blue that is a triangle is a wild bird, and they fly in flocks with a leader. I declare, I've never seen that pattern before. It's very pretty, and, some way, it's just right for our new home in Indiana. We do need quilts, that's a fact! I'll love to have it. Thank you again and again, Lina. I'll use it, and take very, very good care of it until Samanthy moves into a home of her own some day, and then I'll give it to her. How's that?" asked Mother, turning to Samanthy.

"Here come the Fleeners," called James, who had built a fire and had the venison stewing in a big kettle in the yard. Two women, three men, and four children climbed out of the wagon. The men with their axes quickly joined Father, Uncle Sam, Uncle Jake, and David. The women took baskets covered with clean white towels out of the wagon, carried them into the kitchen, and began unpacking them. New bread, hams, fried chicken, and pumpkin pies were piled on the table.

Soon another wagon, and then another turned into the roadway that led to the Calvins' cabin. As Susan watched, several more came into view. Old neighbors, too busy with their own hard duties of pioneer life to take the time for mere social gatherings, were glad to see one another as they helped a new neighbor build a barn, or quilt a patchwork comfort.

At last there were so many people and so many baskets that a long table was set outside and the food placed upon it. In the very middle of the table Mrs. Fleener had put a big fruit pie — the biggest pie Susan had ever seen. Its crust was a beautiful golden brown, and as Samanthy and Susan looked at it closely, they discovered that the top crust formed two large initials W and C.

When the men stopped work on the barn, and the women stopped quilting, the noon dinner was served. As they all sat about the table, Mrs. Fleener said, "There are two letters on this pie — W and C. Whoever guesses what these letters stand for, gets the first piece of pie."

There were many guesses. But it was Samanthy who cried, "I know. Welcome, Calvins!"

Mrs. Fleener beamed as she nodded, and everybody envied Samanthy when she was served with the first big, juicy piece of pie.

After dinner the children played games, the women worked busily on the quilt, and the barn grew from a pile of logs to a building with walls high enough to need only a roof to complete it. Both men and women worked until daylight faded, and the early spring twilight made them think of supper. There were plenty of pies, cakes, and venison stew left, and again they sat around the table eating, and enjoying a friendly visit.

Every crumb of the big pie had been eaten at the noon meal, so at Samanthy's suggestion, Abigail sat smiling in the center of the table. The women admired the fine stitching in her clothes, the men her black leather shoes that would lace and unlace, her portmanteau, and her new hickory bed. Each little girl took turns in holding her, and even the boys noticed her sunbonnet.

When the dishes were washed, and each basket was packed and put back in the family wagon, someone brought out a fiddle. Uncle Jake called, "All take yer partners for a square dance."

Susan, with Abigail in her arms, stood with Samanthy in the doorway of the new home and watched the first set for the square dance form.

Uncle Sam and Mother, Father and Aunt Lina, Mr. and Mrs. Fleener, and finally David, with a very pretty girl dressed in crisp pink gingham, were the ones to dance in the first set. Four more couples joined the dancers, and soon two sets were following Uncle Jake's directions as he called the figures and clapped his hands to accent the rhythm.

CALLS FOR A SQUARE DANCE

Take your partners for a square dance....
First couple balance — swing — out to the right and
Chase the rabbit
Chase the squirrel
Chase the pretty girl round th' world.
Gent drop through, and circle up four,
Lady doe and a gent you know,
Chicken in a bread pan mixing dough.

Out to th' right — swing old Adam,
Now young Eve — now old Adam before you leave.
Back to taw
Cross th' hall and swing Grandmaw.
Back to taw
Cut to th' left — swing your mother in law
Back to taw.

First gent swing — up th' center and break th' ring
—
Right back home.
Swing that gal you swung before,
Up the center and cast off four,
Right back home.
Swing that gal from Kalamazoo,
Up the center and cast off two.
Meet em on th' right — left hand back,
Swing 'em once around — waltz the left hand gal
Same gent swing — up the center and break th'
ring.

"I'm glad you're here, Susan," said Samanthy.

"I'm glad, too," answered Susan simply. Then she slipped in the cabin and placed Abigail and her portmanteau on the mantle, close to the treasured brass candlestick.

As she walked around the dancers, she heard Mother say to Uncle Sam, "I'm very glad we came!"

From where Abigail sat, she gazed through the door at the dancers, swaying, turning, changing partners, all to the gay tune of the fiddle and the calls of Uncle Jake. The fire blazed cheerfully in the big, natural stone fireplace.

From outside came the friendly voices of neighbors laughing together as they waited for a new dance set to form in which they, too, might join. An occasional wagon rattled off in the dusk, the neighbors calling back good-bys, or promising to see one another at meeting on Sunday.

Abigail, happy in her new home in Indiana, sat on the mantle and continued to smile at the friendliness and gaiety about her, with never a backward glance.